I_r

Joseph London
11/19/13

Intravenous

Intravenous

Joseph Landers

Dedication

I'd like to dedicate this book to my wife, who gave me support during the writing process and tirelessly worked as she proofread the novel. She offered suggestions with phasing to help the intended message flow throughout each chapter.

Preface

I come up with the idea for Intravenous because of the recent news coverage related to healthcare reform. Different views were broadcast across television and radio stations, which led to a conglomerate of information being spread to the public but every bit being bias toward the announcer and the station's views.

People without insurance were joyously praising the plan because they thought they could get insurance for free while people with insurance saw it as another tax burden being placed on them.

With the majority of their operating budget coming from the government, hospitals were frantically changing their policies and working standards in an effort to save money because they were unsure how healthcare reform would affect them financially as well as structurally. They believe the government would institute a plan to lower payments for various services, which would lower profits and decrease the money they used to keep the hospital running.

Administrators were continually trying to develop a plan of action to counter the changes that were inevitably going to hit the healthcare industry.

Knowing that a large portion of hospital patients are uninsured and have no way of paying their bill and taking the current changes that the hospitals faced into consideration, I developed a totally fictional story which put those fears together and *Intravenous* was born.

Introduction

It was a stressful day at Westbrook Medical Center as the hospital's directors studied page upon page of financial records trying to develop a plan to save revenue and keep the hospital afloat. Payments from the government were three months behind, and when they arrived the hospital only received a small portion of the bill. This was a way for the government to cut expenses and lower the total amount allocated for healthcare costs.

Private insurance companies discovered this technique and implemented it in their billing practices themselves, which further decreased operational money for the hospital, thus leaving the hospital with an even bigger deficit.

With the decrease in revenue, the hospital was unable to buy improvements and therefore they had to work with substandard equipment. The supplies they ordered were the cheapest they could buy, which meant they were irregular and second quality items. Nurses had to go through several IV pumps to get one that would work, medications were being selectively ordered, and blood was being rationed to the most critical cases.

Westbrook Medical Center was facing dire days. Without a drastic change the hospital would soon be a thing of the past.

Larry Adcock, CEO of Westbrook Medical Center, laid the stack of papers he was holding down, looked across the table and asked in a stress filled voice, "Has anyone got a suggestion?"

"Whatever we do, we must not let the press get wind of our financial situation," Hanna Johns, Chief Nursing Officer for Westbrook Medical Center, insisted. "We must keep a good image for the hospital or patients will stop coming in and we won't have any revenue."

"What about staffing?" Willie Pike, Chief of Staff for the hospital, asked. "Can we cut the nurses?"

"We changed their numbers after you suggested it at our last meeting," Hanna Johns replied dryly as she looked around the table then added, "Staffing numbers have been cut to the point that each floor looks vacant throughout the night. Nurses now have seven to eight patients each. Sometimes they work with a tech, but most nights they don't and on most floors a unit secretary is a distant memory. Remember we still need to keep our patient satisfaction scores up or the government will decrease the amount they pay us even more."

"What else can you do?" Larry Adcock asked.

"I guess we could cut hospital maintenance," Willie Pike spoke up.

"They've already been cut to a four day work week," Hanna Johns pointed out as she looked at the minutes from last week's meeting.

After scratching his head, Larry Adcock announced, "Let's just keep things the way they are for now and see if the budget improves over the next few weeks," then he stood up and said, "Keep thinking of ways to improve the hospital," and he walked out the door.

"I still don't see why we can't cut the nurses," Willie Pike grumbled.

"Right now the nurses are responsible for everything. They round on the patients only when they have to, and the rest of the time they stay at the desk so they can complete the charting that is required of them. Remember if they don't chart it, we can't prove it happened and the government won't pay for services not charted," Hanna shot back. "The last time I went to a floor at night, the lights were turned low to enhance an environment for the patients to sleep. This made the halls ominous, but it helped everyone get their work done. When the nurses talked they spoke in a low tone for fear of waking the patients and creating more work. I'd say they've been cut as much as can safely be done."

"What about hospital security?" Willie asked.

"We've cut our security staff in half for each shift," Gus Mills, Head of Security spoke up, "But we've strategically placed them in various areas to keep the hospital safe."

"And you're sure the hospital is safe?" Hanna asked.

"I'd bet my life on it," Gus replied. "It's just as safe as it was before the cuts," he reinforced confidently, as they walked out the door.

Chapter 1

A darkly clothed figure stood behind a door that had been left ajar. It was the only empty room on the third floor of Westbrook Medical Center. He watched as the nurses passed out their nightly medication, each nurse staying about five minutes with a patient before moving to the next.

Anticipation grew as Rose Miller, one of the nightshift nurses, went into the target's room and lingered for what seemed like an hour before emerging with a garbage bag full of linens. She took it to the utility room, tossed it inside, and went back to the nurses' station.

Peggy Farris, certified nursing technician, followed along behind the nurses doing midnight vital signs at ten o'clock in an attempt at giving the patients a few hours to sleep before four o'clock vitals were due and morning labs were to be drawn.

The hidden man watched as Peggy finished with the vital signs and smiled to himself knowing that the patients would not be checked on for a couple of hours, which would be plenty of time to complete the task at hand.

At ten thirty, Peggy finished with the last patient, and then she parked the portable machine against the wall and walked back to the nurses' station.

When she got there she found everyone gathered around the desk discussing what they wanted to eat for supper and from which restaurant they were going to order.

After several minutes, the decision was made and everyone moved away from the nurse's desk. Each nurse settled in front of a computer with their backs toward the hall to start charting on their patients while Peggy Farris and Vicki Henson, the unit secretary, went into the break room to watch television while they waited for their food to arrive.

From his hiding place, the man waited five minutes, straightening the wrinkles out of his dark blue scrubs, then slowly emerged from the empty room and walked to the target's door.

After glancing down the hall to make sure no one had noticed him, he knocked on the door and quietly slipped inside the target's room.

"Who are you?" the target asked in a medicine- induced sleepy voice.

"Rose had a family emergency and had to leave, so I'm taking over her patients," he said in a matter of fact way. "I'll be your nurse for the rest of the night."

The target looked at him suspiciously and said, "I've been here awhile. I've never seen you here before."

"This is my first shift this week," he responded, as he smiled. "I work the next two nights."

"Well, I knew I'd never seen you," the target said feeling a little more relaxed.

"You won't see me much tonight, because I'm going to let you sleep after I give you this medicine."

"I've already had my medicine for tonight," the target said, as she looked at the syringe in the intruder's right hand.

"This is not one of your scheduled medicines. This was just ordered by the doctor as a onetime dose to be given tonight."

"What is it?"

"Lorazepam."

"What's it for?"

"It will help you relax, so you can get a good night's sleep."

"I was almost asleep when you walked in the room."

"I'm sorry, but you have a big day planned tomorrow and your doctor thinks you need this to rest."

"Alright, give it to me so I can get some sleep," the target conceded, as she pulled her arm from under the cover and held it out.

"This may burn a little," the killer said and moved closer to the target.

After attaching the syringe to the IV tubing, he looked around the bed and spotted an extra pillow lying in a chair beside the patient.

"Let me make you more comfortable," the intruder said, as he got the pillow off the chair and began fluffing it up.

"I'm alright the way I am," the target said irritably. "Just give me the medicine."

"Alright, I'll be happy to," the lone figure said, as he took the syringe and slowly began pushing the medicine into the IV.

"That burns!" the target yelled.

"It'll be over before you know it," he said, as he quickly placed the pillow over the target's mouth and pressed it tightly.

The target fought violently to get the pillow off of her face. She attempted to kick her killer with her legs, but she was unable to raise them off of the bed. She grabbed her killer's shirt with her right hand and pulled toward her, but she was no match for the lone figure's strength.

He braced the pillow with his left hand and stretched his right toward the IV tubing. After much effort, he took the syringe and finished pushing the rest of the medicine into the target's vein with one quick push.

Within seconds of the medication being given, the target stopped fighting and her body went limp. She slumped over in the bed with her head resting against the side rail at an awkward angle and her eyes open staring at nothingness.

The lone figure threw the pillow back into the chair where he had gotten it and discarded the empty syringe in the sharps container. Then he turned and stood looking over the target's lifeless body for several seconds. He smiled with satisfaction and walked out the door.

As he got in the hall, the killer looked at the nurses' station to make sure no one was watching. No one was in sight, so he walked to the stairs, quietly opened the door and slipped inside.

Chapter 2

Jeff Bishop, the floor's charge nurse, ran down the hall as he heard Rose Miller scream, "Code 10 in room 348!"

When Jeff got close to the door, he could see Rose leaning over the body of a small frail lady in her late eighties trying to get her to respond. She vigorously rubbed the lady's sternum with her knuckles, but the lady didn't respond. She quickly collapsed the mattress and started chest compressions.

"What happened?" Jeff asked, as he grabbed the ambu bag off the wall and ran to the head of the bed.

"When I came to check on her, she was slumped over and unresponsive," Rose explained. "She was fine two hours ago when I gave her meds to her."

"Sometimes this happens," Jeff said, as he connected the ambu bag to oxygen and started giving breaths after each cycle of chest compressions.

As they worked Jeff could hear the crash cart clanging as it rolled down the hall toward where they were frantically working to keep the lady's lifeless body oxygenated by using CPR.

Jeff watched as Emma Freeman pushed the crash cart into

the room and plugged the defibrillator into the wall socket. Then she attached the defibrillator pads on the frail lady's chest and turned the monitor on to analyze her heart rhythm.

Rose stopped chest compressions as the monitor came to life and they watched as a straight line ran across the monitor indicating that the lady's heart wasn't beating. Then she started back pumping on the lady's chest.

"Is she a full code?" Jeff asked.

"She has terminal cancer, but she and her family still wanted everything done," Rose answered.

"Then we will do everything we can to save her," he said and gave two breaths.

Jeff looked up as two doctors and a respiratory therapist rushed into the room.

The respiratory therapist skirted around the crash cart and moved to the head of the bed where he was standing. She got in position to take the ambu bag and continue respirations without interrupting the process. Then she said, "I'll take over," as she took the ambu bag.

Sonya McGee, one of the doctors who had walked into the room and who happened to be chief resident of the medical service covering the patient asked, "What happened?" Then she moved toward the lady's chest and added, "I'll take over with the compressions," and she started pushing on the lady's chest.

"She was fine at ten o'clock when I gave her meds," Rose said as she took a step back.

"Do we have IV access?" Sonya asked.

Jeff looked at the lady's right forearm, which had an IV and studied it for a few seconds before saying, "She has a twenty in her left arm, but it doesn't look very good. It has red streaks running up toward her elbow," and he looked at

Rose and asked, "What did you have infusing through this IV?"

"I only gave her Vancomycin," Rose said.

Sonya looked at the resident that followed her in the room and said, "Start a central line so we can start giving her some meds."

"I need a central line kit," the resident stated to the nurse at the crash cart.

Emma opened the third drawer on the crash cart, took a central line kit out, and handed it to the resident. Then she got a package of size seven sterile gloves and laid them on the bed.

"Where do you want me to put it?" the resident asked.

"In her groin," Sonya said.

The resident instantly put her hand on the lady's groin and started feeling for a pulse. "Hey, I feel a pulse!" she exclaimed.

"It's the chest compression that's giving you the pulse," Sonya said, "Not her heart beat."

"Oh," she said and began concentrating on where to place the central line.

She found her mark and began cleaning the site. After the site was cleaned with betadine, she inserted the needle to find the vein. She worked the needle back and forth several times before getting a blood return, and then she carefully threaded the plastic cannula over the wire until the central line was ready to be sutured in place.

When the line was secured, the resident pulled back several vials of blood and handed them to Jeff.

"What labs do you want?" Jeff asked.

The resident looked at Sonya without saying anything.

"CBC, FMP with magnesium and calcium, PT, PTT, and

Ammonia," Sonya said, as she looked at the resident and frowned.

"I got it," Jeff said and ran out the door.

"Is the line ready to us?" Sonya asked.

"Yes, it's ready," the resident said. "Do you want me to push atropine?"

"No, the new guidelines are for epinephrine instead of atropine," Sonya said "Give 1 mg of epinephrine."

The pharmacist had slipped in while the resident was starting the central line and was waiting on which drugs they wanted to administer. As Sonya gave the order for epinephrine, the pharmacist had the drug drawn up and was ready for the resident to administer the drug. "Here it is," he said as he handed the syringe to the resident.

The resident took the syringe and pushed the medication through the central line while Sonya and the respiratory therapist continued CPR. After they completed the cycle they paused for a few seconds to see if the patient's heart had started beating. Then they started back after no heartbeat was detected.

After another cycle of CPR Sonya barked, "Give another milligram of epinephrine!"

As soon as the pharmacist pulled up the drug, the resident took the syringe filled with epinephrine and quickly pushed it into the patient's central line.

They performed CPR for about a minute to make sure the medicine had completely been circulated throughout the patient's body. Then they stopped to reevaluate for a heartbeat. Still no heartbeat, so they resumed CPR.

After several more cycles with little effect, Jeff rushed into the room and announced, "I have the lab results."

"I need someone to relieve me so I can look at the results," Sonya said, as she moved to the side of the patient to let someone get into position to perform chest compression.

"I will," Rose said as she stepped beside Sonya and started chest compressions.

Sonya looked at the labs. She then looked at Jeff and asked, "Was the blood hemolyzed."

"No, it wasn't," Jeff said.

"Stop the code," Sonya announced. "I'm calling it."

"Why?" the resident asked.

"Her potassium is 12.6," Sonya said. "No one can live with their potassium 12.6. Her heart is shot."

Rose stopped chest compressions.

The respiratory therapist stopped giving breaths. "I need to get to my floor and start my treatments," she said, as she walked out the door.

Rose looked at Sonya and said, "Her potassium was 3.7 this morning. How could it have climbed that high without her getting potassium?"

"I don't know," Sonya said as she walked to the door and turned and added, "Leave everything in place while I call the family and see if they want an autopsy," and she walked out the door.

Rose stopped the IV pump and covered the body with a sheet. Then she started cleaning up the room.

Emma put the defibrillator back on the crash cart and pushed it out of the room. She parked it away from the room so the family wouldn't see it when they came to view the body.

Rose came out of the room, closed the door, walked to the desk, and sat down to wait for the doctor to say if the family wanted an autopsy or not.

Chapter 3

I was called at three thirty in the morning to come to the hospital to investigate the suspicious death of a patient. My name is Ted Maxwell. I'm in charge of patient safety at Westbrook Medical Center, which is a four hundred bed for profit hospital located on the southwest side of Oregon. Our patient population generally comes from southern Washington, northern California, and western Oregon.

I have an associate's degree in nursing, but have worked my way up the ladder by performing different jobs and showing competency in whatever jobs I'm asked to do. At Westbrook Medical Center you aren't judged by the number of letters you have behind your name, but by how well you do your job.

After working for the hospital for twenty years, I accepted the job as patient safety officer ten years ago when the hospital's CEO Larry Adcock approached me and expressed his concerns over an increase in medical errors and asked me to take on a new roll. I had just recently married my wife Sara, and the new job would mean more money and guaranteed weekends off. Now that we have our children,

John 8, Mark 6, and Mary 3, it's even more important that I have the weekends free to devote to my family.

As I said before, I'm in charge of patient safety, and I investigate every patient death. Most of the time, I'm looking at charts. Tonight however, I was called to the floor because this patient's death was unusual due to the extremely elevated potassium level.

When I reached the floor, I was met by Rose Miller and Jeff Bishop before I got to the nursing station.

"Hey Ted," Jeff said when he approached.

"Hey Jeff," I said and looked at Rose and added, "Hi Rose."

"Hi," she said in a low voice.

"What's the patient's name?" I asked.

"Doris Moore," Rose said.

"Can you tell me a little bit about her?"

"Sure," Rose said, as she looked at a sheet of paper she had in her hand and added, "She was eighty six years old. She had stage 4 liver cancer which metastasized to the lungs and spleen. They also found several small lesions in her brain."

"Who found the patient?" I asked.

"I did," Rose said.

"When was the last time you saw her alive?"

"I gave her meds at about nine thirty, and Peggy did her vital signs at ten o'clock," she said and added, "She was alive at that time."

"What meds did you give her?"

"Let's see, she had Metoprolol, Trazodone, OxyContin, and Vancomycin."

"None of those medications should elevate her potassium."

"I know. That's why I don't understand why it was so

high."

"Is her body still in the room?"

"Yes, we're still waiting on some of the family to come by and see the body before we can wrap it."

"Did they request an autopsy?"

"No. They said they didn't want one."

"Great, that means I'll need to talk them into allowing us to perform one so we can find out how she died."

"I know how she died," Jeff said. "Her potassium was 12.6."

"I understand that," I said. "But I want to find out what happened to make it that high."

"And you think an autopsy will give you the answer."

"We won't know unless we do one."

"What if they refuse?" Rose asked, as she looked down the hall at one of the family members that had stepped out of the room and was standing by the door.

"I'll cross that bridge when I come to it," I said, as I walked away from Rose and approached the family member that was standing in the hall.

When I got close, he turned to me and halfway smiled.

I stuck my hand out and said, "My name is Ted Maxwell. I'm in charge of patient safety for the hospital." Then I added in a consoling voice, "I'm sorry for your loss."

The man shook my hand and said, "I'm George Moore her nephew," and smiled sadly as he said, "She lived a long and happy life."

"Are you the next of kin?"

"No, her daughter is still in the room saying goodbye," he said, as he pointed to the door and asked, "Do you want me to get her?"

"No, I can wait until she's through," I said and glanced at

the clock on the wall.

"Let me get her, or she'll be in there for hours," he said, as he opened the door and asked, "Aunt Mary, are you ready to leave?"

A small lady in her late fifties walked to the door and said, "I guess I am," and she looked back at the body lying on the bed before walking out the door into the hall.

"This man works for the hospital and he has something he wants to ask you," George said as he pointed toward me.

I stepped forward, stuck my hand out and said, "I'm Ted Maxwell."

"I'm Gladys Hunt," the lady said as she took my hand and asked, "What do you need son?"

"We would like to do an autopsy on your mother to see if we can find what happened and hopefully prevent it from happening again."

"I thought she died from a complication of her cancer."

"That well may be, but we won't know for sure without an autopsy."

"And you say this might help someone else?"

"It might."

"Okay, you can do your autopsy, but then I want my mother's body."

"Can I get you to sign this form stating that you're giving us permission to do the autopsy?" I asked and handed her a clipboard with the consent for autopsy attached.

She took the clipboard, studied it for a few seconds, and then she signed the consent. After looking at the consent one more time, she handed it to me and asked, "Is that everything you need?"

I took the clipboard and glanced at the signature, which was squiggly but discernible. "There is one more thing," I said as I took my notepad out of my pocket.

"What is it?" she asked a little impatiently.

"What funeral home do you want her body sent to?"

"I want you to send her to Griffin's Funeral Home on Cobb Street."

"Please give us a day to do the autopsy, and we'll have her at the funeral home early in the morning."

"Alright," she said, as she turned to George and said, "Let's go," and she walked away.

George looked at me, and then he followed her down the hall toward the elevators.

I watched as they turned the corner and disappeared. Then I went to the phone and called the morgue to arrange for the body to be picked up. I also informed the attendant that an autopsy needed to be performed as soon as possible and then the body should be sent to Griffin Funeral Home.

After I hung the phone up, I went into the patient's room to get a look at her body before the morgue attendant arrived. I kept her body covered with the sheet. Only lifting the corners that I felt I needed to. I uncovered her head so I could see her face, which revealed the beginning of rigor mortis. Then I moved to her arm that had the IV and lifted the sheet to get a better look. I immediately noticed the red streaks running up her arm toward her elbow.

After putting the sheet back in place, I turned to the IV pole and studied the fluids that had been connected to the patient before she died. I saw a large bag of 9% normal saline and a small bag with Vancomycin 1000 mg written across the front of the bag. I looked at the IV pump, which indicated that the infusing volume was 100 ml an hour.

Nothing I saw would cause the lady's death, so I walked out the door and went to my office to wait on the autopsy report.

Chapter 4

At eleven thirty Dr. Garland Bennett, the hospital's pathologist in charge of performing autopsies on patients that die in the hospital, was sitting in my office. A manila envelope was lying across his thighs. The envelope contained the results of the autopsy that he had performed on Doris Moore.

He took a sip of coffee, sat the cup on the table beside him and said, "Let's get started with this report," as he opened the manila envelope and slid the contents out into his hand.

"Could you tell if the hospital caused her death?" I asked.

"Let me tell you the results, and then you and I can try to decide," he said, as he looked at the top sheet of paper. "She had cancer which had progressed to be classified as stage 4 that affected her liver, lungs, and spleen. I also found several small lesions in her brain. She had the beginning stages of pneumonia in her left lower lobe."

"What about her heart?" I asked with anticipation.

He looked at me for a few seconds and said, "Her left ventricle was enlarged almost to the point of not functioning, and she had severe congestive heart failure," and he shifted his position in his chair then added, "She also had a blood clot in her left lower extremity."

"What killed her?"

"Nothing that I mentioned killed her."

"Then how did she die?"

"Her heart stopped beating."

"Were you able to tell why her heart stopped beating?"

"According to the labs that were drawn during the code, her potassium level was 12.6," he said., "A high concentration of potassium in your blood can cause your heart to short circuit which can cause the nerves and muscles to malfunction. This can lead to palpitations or irregular heart rate. If the levels continue to increase, it could lead to heart failure and eventually asystole."

"Did you run any test on her blood?"

"Yes, I ran levels on her blood to recheck them with what was drawn during the code," he said and looked at the report in his hand. "Her potassium dropped to 10.8, but that could have been due to the fluids that were administered during the code."

"Why do you think her potassium was so high?"

"I don't know," he said. "I checked the bag of 9% normal saline that was hanging to make sure nothing had been added to the fluid, and I also checked the empty bag that was hanging on the pole, but I didn't find any potassium in either bag."

"What about her IV?"

"Something caustic was infused through the IV," he said, as he slid to the edge of his chair and added, "Vancomycin can cause redness if it's infused too fast or if it is not deluded enough, but not to the extent that I saw. I suspect that someone infused potassium through that IV at a rapid rate."

"Are you saying that she was murdered?"

He shrugged his shoulders and said, "My report will state that she died because her heart stopped beating since I can't prove anything else."

I relaxed a little and said, "So, you're basically going to document the facts and not speculate on the cause of death."

"My job is to find the facts and report them as they are," he said, as he looked in my eyes and added, "It would be unprofessional to state my opinion in the report."

"Can I have a copy of the autopsy report?" I asked. "I would like to keep a copy on file in my office."

"This is yours," he said, as he got up and laid the contents on the manila envelope on my desk. "Call me if you have any questions," and he walked out the door.

I took the autopsy report and put it back in the manila envelope. Then I opened my top drawer and dropped it inside. I closed the drawer, locked it, and put the keys inside my filing cabinet.

Before sitting down, I looked at the clock and saw it was lunchtime. I leaned over my desk and looked at my calendar. The meeting I had arranged with the staff that was working when Doris Moore died was two hours away, so I decided to go to lunch. I walked out of my office, closing the door and locking it before I went to the cafeteria.

Chapter 5

Rose Miller was the first person to come to my office. I looked up at the open door and watched as she hesitated for a few seconds before gently knocking.

"Come in," I said as I pointed at a chair that I had placed at my desk for this interview and said, "Have a seat."

She looked around the room before sitting down. Then she slid the chair close to my desk and sat her purse on the floor beside her. After repositioning in the chair, she looked me in the eyes and asked, "What do you want to know?"

I looked at my notepad where I had jotted down a few notes from the night before and asked, "Did you give Mrs. Moore any potassium last night?"

"No, I did not," she said in a matter of fact way.

"Did you see anyone go into her room other than yourself?"

"After I gave Mrs. Moore her meds, Peggy Farris went in to do her vital signs."

"Did Peggy have anything unusual with her when she went into the room?"

"I didn't notice," she said, "I was busy giving meds."

"Do you have any idea what happened to Mrs. Moore's IV site?"

"I mixed her Vancomycin in 100 ml of normal saline like I'm supposed to, and I let it run over an hour and fifteen minutes to make sure I didn't run it too fast," she said, as she leaned forward and added, "That was all I put through her IV."

"Was it red after you gave her the Vancomycin?"

"It may have had some slight redness, but nothing like what I saw when we coded her."

"What do you think caused the redness?"

"I have no idea."

"Did you see anyone suspicious on the floor?"

"No."

"Is there anything you can tell me about last night that I haven't asked?"

"I've told you everything I know," she said as she reached down and picked up her purse and asked, "Can I go now?"

"Sure," I said as I glanced at the door and added, "Send Jeff in if he is out there."

"I will," she said, as she got up and walked out the door.

Within seconds, Jeff Bishop was standing at the door. He stopped at the entrance and asked, "Are you ready to see me?"

"Yes, come on in Jeff and have a seat," I said and pointed at the chair in which Rose had been sitting.

He casually walked to the chair and sat down. He slumped over a little as he tried to get comfortable then straightened up and asked, "What's going on Ted?"

"I have to follow up on some things from last night," I said.

"Alright, what do you want to know?"

"How long have you known Rose Miller?"

"About three years."

"Would you classify her as a good nurse?"

"I think she is a good nurse," Jeff said and then asked, "What are you getting at?"

"I'm just trying to get a feel of her character."

"If I were in the hospital, I would let her take care of me," Jeff said. "She takes good care of her patients."

"When did you first go into Mrs. Moore's room?"

"When Rose called a code."

"What was Rose doing when you went into the room?"

"She was trying to arouse her by doing a sternal rub then she started chest compressions."

"Did you see her put anything into Mrs. Moore's IV?"

"No," Jeff said, as he raised his voice. "You can forget about Rose hurting her patients because she takes very good care of them and takes it personally if something bad happens."

"Alright," I said, "I was just trying to understand her a little more."

"I can tell you that she didn't hurt Mrs. Moore."

"That's good to know," I said and changed the questioning a little by asking, "Did you see anyone unusual on the floor last night?"

"No. Not that I can remember."

"You were in charge last night weren't you?"

"Yes, I was in charge," Jeff said. "Where are you going with this?"

"I was just thinking that you're responsible for whatever happens on the floor."

"I feel bad about what happened last night, but we didn't do anything to cause it and we did everything we could to bring her back."

"Do you have any idea how her potassium got so high?"

"I wouldn't know," Jeff said a little perturbed.

"Alright, then that's all the questions I have right now," I said. "Please send Peggy in if she is in the lobby."

"I'll do it," Jeff said and he walked out the door.

Peggy stuck her head in my office and asked, "Hi, you ready to see me?"

"Come on in and have a seat," I said as I turned the page on my notepad.

Peggy nervously stepped toward the chair. She stumbled slightly as she stepped in front of my desk but regained her balance and sat down. She looked at the floor but decided to put her purse on her lap instead of sitting it on the floor beside her legs. Then she cleared her throat and asked, "Why did you want to see me?"

"It's just a formality," I said, as I got up and closed the door.

She took a deep breath and slowly let it out as she tried to relax.

"I have a few questions I need to clarify," I said, as I sat down and jotted nervous on the notepad.

"What kind of questions?"

"I understand that you were the last person to see Mrs. Moore alive," I said and looked Peggy in the eyes.

Her face began to turn red. She looked down at her purse, shifted its position, and said, "I don't know what you've heard, but I had nothing to do with that woman's death."

"What do you mean?"

"Her daughter complained to the nurse manager that I didn't come the minute she called for the bedpan," she said, as she looked at me testily, and added, "I was in another patient's room when she called. I finished what I was doing with that patient then I went to help her on the bedpan, but she had already wet the bed."

"What did your nurse manager say?"

"She said we were sorry and would try to do better the next time."

"What did she say to you?"

"She asked me what happened and when I explained what had happened she said it couldn't have been avoided."

"Were you angry at her?"

"No, I saw her point but I was doing the best I could."

"Did she say anything to you?"

"Not a word."

"Did Mrs. Moore seem to be in any distress when you did her vital signs?"

"I would have told Rose if she had been."

"Thanks for your time," I said as I got up and opened the door.

"Is that it?" Peggy asked as she stood up.

"Right now, that's all the questions I have."

"Alright," she said and walked out the door.

I watched her leave. Then I closed my office door and put the notepad away. I booted my computer up and began typing a report on my findings, which would be filed with the autopsy report for later reference if needed.

Chapter 6

A dark figure stood in the shadows of John Moss' room listening to him labor to breathe under the expanded mask with one hundred percent oxygen flowing toward his nose and mouth. Gasping with each breathe, Moss' body heaved as he expelled air, then fell limp from the energy it took. His oxygen monitor indicated that he was getting enough oxygen to survive, but the monitor didn't calculate the energy expended to maintain that level.

The dark figure, cloaked behind the privacy curtain, watched as a young female dressed in scrubs walked into the room to give medicine to the target. She mixed several crushed pills with water and pushed them down a tube that was protruding out of his nose. Then she took a syringe out of her pocket and pushed some medicine in his IV line. After she finished, she looked at the IV pump to check the settings and then walked out of the door.

After she left, the dark figure silently moved toward the IV pump that was infusing several different medications through a central line located in the target's neck. According to the bottles hanging, he had nitroglycerine infusing at 3cc an hour, heparin sodium infusion at 22cc an hour and 5% dextrose in water infusing at 75cc an hour.

A Foley catheter was hanging on the side of the bed. A compression devise was wrapped around his legs in an attempt at preventing blood clots. He had both of his arms elevated on pillows to decrease the swelling and promote circulation.

The dark figure stopped the IV pump that had nitroglycerine and heparin infusing. Then he opened the side door and removed the tubing connected to the nitroglycerine. After looking at the control panel on the tubing, he opened the flow valve and let the nitro infuse into his target as fast as it could drip. After several minutes, the dark figure reattached the IV tubing to the pump and restarted the nitroglycerine and heparin at the rates they had previously been running.

Satisfied with his accomplishment, he went to the foot of the bed and watched as John Moss' blood pressure slowly began to drop until it was probably irreversible then he eased out the door. No one was in the hall, so he quickly walked to the stairs, quietly opened the door, and slipped off the unit.

Chapter 7

"What's going on with your patient in bed twelve?" Bill asked, as he pointed to the monitor which indicated that the patient's blood pressure was seventy- six over forty- five.

Susan Brunner got up and walked to the monitor. "I don't know. He's been running in the 120's most of the night," she said, as a look of concern came over her face. "I guess I need to turn off his nitro drip and see if that will bring his pressure back up," and she quickly walked around the desk and hastily went down the hall.

When she entered the room, she first checked the blood pressure cuff to make sure it was properly attached to his arm. After verifying the cuff was in place, she stopped the nitroglycerine drip and pushed start on the control panel of the monitor to recheck his blood pressure.

This time his pressure had dropped to 69 over 39. She grabbed a bag of normal saline out of the storage bin, attached tubing and began infusing it through his central line as fast as it could infuse.

"Do you need help?" Bill asked, as he walked in the room.

"I'm not sure yet," she said. "I stopped his nitro and am

giving him a bolus of normal saline."

"Is he septic?"

"He might be, but he hasn't been showing any signs of septicemia until now," she said as she hit the button to recheck his blood pressure again and conceded, "I think he may have gotten too much nitro."

They watched as the blood pressure cuff expanded then slowly started to relax as it clicked down to measure his blood pressure and 59 over 35 flashed on the screen.

"Call Doctor Dutton, and let her know what is happening," Bill said. "I'll stay with the patient while you're making the call." He grabbed another bag of normal saline and replaced the empty bag that had infused. He then lowered the head of the bed, with the feet raised, putting the patient in the Trendelenburg position.

Bill took the bag and began squeezing it with his hands, forcing the fluid into the central line in an attempt to increase the patient's pressure. As the bag quickly emptied, Bill grabbed another bag and turned the fluid control to a slow drip.

Susan rushed to the phone and dialed the number to the doctor's call room. The phone rang several times before a sleepy voice said, "Yes, what's going on?"

Susan said, "Doctor Dutton, bed twelve's pressure has dropped to 59 over 35."

"Did you stop the nitro?"

"Yes, I've stopped the nitro and we've given him a bolus of normal saline."

"I'll be there in a minute," Doctor Dutton said and hung up the phone.

Susan put the phone down and went back to her patient's room to recheck his vital signs.

When she entered the room Bill said, "He's had two liters of normal saline. I'm almost afraid he might get fluid overload."

"Let me check his vital signs, so I can have them ready when Doctor Dutton gets here," Susan said, as she reached up and hit the start button on the monitor. He had a thermometer attached to his Foley catheter, which would give the internal temperature of his bladder.

Lynn Dutton is a fellow who is specializing in respiratory care. Part of her training includes pulling shifts in the medical intensive care unit. She arrived on the floor less than two minutes after Susan informed her of John Moss' dropping blood pressure and went straight into his room.

"Did his blood pressure get any better?" she asked as she walked in the room.

Susan looked at the monitor as the vital signs popped on the screen. She recited, "Blood pressure 75 over 52, heart rate 98, respirations 26 and labored and his temperature 97.6."

"His blood pressure increased a little after he got normal saline," she added.

"How much fluid did he get?" Dr. Dutton asked.

"He is getting his third liter of fluid," Bill said.

"What was his pressure when you started the fluid?" she asked.

"His pressure was 59 over 35," Susan said.

"How much nitro was he getting?"

"He was getting 3cc an hour."

Dr. Dutton looked at the medicines hanging on the IV pole. She looked at the heparin, then at the dextrose and water. She put her hand on the bag that contained the nitroglycerine and studied it for a few seconds. "He might have just gotten too much nitro," she said, as she let go on the bag. "Give him another liter of normal saline and keep a close eye on his pressure," Dr. Dutton said. "We may have to start Dopamine."

"Do you want me to bolus him?" Susan asked.

"No, infuse it at 250cc an hour," she said. "I don't want to fluid overload him. If his pressure starts to drop give me a call and we'll start him on Dopamine," and she walked out of the room.

Susan placed the normal saline on the pump and set it to run at 250cc an hour. Then she set the monitor to do vital signs every five minutes and stood watching as the first set was done.

She smiled as her patient's blood pressure rose to 83 over 58. After looking one more time at the pump to make sure everything was set right, she walked back to the nurses desk and sat down to chart what had just taken place.

Bill followed Susan out of the room, but he went to check on his patients before going to the desk to chart.

Chapter 8

Leo Brown was stocking the clean supply room on Three North with the items that had been ordered by the unit secretary the previous day. He stocked the IV catheters, bedpans, packs of 4x4 gauge, and rolls and rolls of tape. Some silk, some paper, and some clear plastic. As he stocked the shelf, he checked each item off a sheet of paper to make sure the proper amount had been sent to last throughout the next day.

After he finished with the small items, he started on the large boxes of IV fluids. He had two boxes of normal saline, two boxes of half normal saline, and a box mixed with various different fluids that are not used as often.

When he finished, he looked at his cart, which had a pile of empty boxes to be sent back to the warehouse to be recycled and noticed another box of normal saline at the end of the cart. He studied his list.

Every item had a check by it, which meant he had delivered everything that had been ordered. He looked at the extra box and decided to put the bags of fluid in the bin so he wouldn't have to carry it back to the warehouse.

Leo reached down and grabbed the seam to rip the box open but the seal had already been broken. A full box of normal saline would normally be sealed, but maybe someone accidentally opened it and sat it on the wrong cart.

He didn't care what happened. He just knew that he didn't want to carry anything back to the warehouse, so he threw the bags of fluid in the bin with the other bags of normal saline and sat the empty box on his cart with the rest of the boxes to be recycled.

Leo thought, 'We've probably shorted this floor before so this time I'll give them a little extra.' Then he lined the boxes up so they would fit through the door and walked out. He stopped at the nurses' desk and got the unit secretary to sign his supply sheet. Then he left the floor without mentioning the extra box of IV fluid he had put in the supply room.

Chapter 9

Bert Summerland was lying in his hospital bed watching the local news when he touched the end of his nose and said, "I must be catching a cold because my nose is running."

Carol Summerland, his wife, shivered and said, "It is probably because this room is so cold," and continued watching television.

"My nose is bleeding," he exclaimed, as a drop of blood ran down his arm.

"Have you been picking your nose?" she asked.

"No, I haven't been picking my nose," he said and added sarcastically, "I'm not ten years old anymore."

"I didn't mean anything by it," she said defensively, "Usually your nose doesn't start bleeding without something causing it to start."

"Well, mine did," he said, "Can you give me a tissue so I can catch it before it drips on the bed?"

"Sure," she said and she handed him a box of hospital tissues.

"As scratchy as these things are they might make it bleed more," he said and pulled a tissue from the box.

"Maybe not," Carol said, as she looked toward him and asked, "Do you want me to call your nurse?"

"Not right now," he said, as he pinched his nose tight. "Maybe it will stop in a little bit."

"Alright, just let me know if you change your mind," Carol said as she turned back to the television.

About twenty minutes later Bert looked at his IV and said, "My IV seems to be burning more than it was before."

Carol got up and looked at the IV that was in Bert's left forearm. She rubbed around the catheter tip and said, "It doesn't look swollen."

"I guess it is just my imagination," Bert said as he moved the tissue away from his nose and a drop of blood fell to his chest.

"I'm going to get the nurse," Carol said with authority. "Your nose should have stopped bleeding by now," and she walked out the door.

She turned right when she got in the hall and walked toward the nurses' station. When she got to the desk, she looked from one person to another until she spotted her husband's nurse then she moved around the desk to be closer to where the nurse was sitting.

Christine Eaton was in the process of charting her daily assessment when she felt the presence of someone standing over her. She signed her documentation then glanced up and smiled as she recognized one of her patient's family members standing in front of her.

She grabbed her paper work that had the information on her patients and asked, "Can I help you?"

"Yes," the lady said, "I'm Bert Summerland's wife, and he needs to see you."

"Is there something wrong?"

"He has a nose bleed."

"Has he held pressure?"

"He's held pressure for about thirty minutes, but it's still bleeding."

"Give me a minute, and I'll come in his room," Christine said, as she click onto his profile and began scanning over his morning lab results. His labs were fine, so she got up and walked to his room.

When she entered she saw the blood drenched tissue in his right hand.

"How long have you been bleeding?" she asked.

"About thirty-five minutes," Bert said.

Christine put on a pair of gloves and stepped up beside him. She moved the bedside table over so she could get a better look at his nose. Then she assessed his eyes, which were extremely bloodshot, but nothing was oozing from his pores. To better see, she turned the overhead light on and instantly took a deep breathe when she saw a small trail of blood seeping out of his right ear.

Trying to stay calm she backed up toward the door and said, "I'm going to call the doctor, and let him know that your nose is bleeding. He might want us to draw some labs," and she walked out the door.

When she got to the nurses' desk, she paged the resident on call and waited by the desk for an answer. After several minutes with no answer, she paged the resident again.

Instead of the resident calling her back, he walked up and demanded, "Who is Christine?" then announced imperially, "We are trying to round."

Christine smiled at the resident and said calmly, "I need you to go see Bert Summerland."

"We'll see him when we round," he said.

"His nose is bleeding, and he has blood coming out of his right ear."

"He probably scratched himself," he said. "We'll be in his room in a few minutes," and he walked away.

The resident stopped and turned as Carol Summerland ran into the hall and yelled, "Help! My husband is vomiting blood! I need a doctor and I need one now!" She looked at the resident that had stopped walking, and she demanded, "Get in here now!"

His face reddened, but he ran into the room without saying another word.

Christine followed.

"Get the crash cart!" he yelled when he got in the room.

Christine ran to the crash cart and pushed it toward the room.

Robert Horton, one of the registered nurses on the floor picked up the phone and told the operator to announce a code 10 over the loud speaker. Then he ran into the room, which was already filled with the team of doctors that was covering the patient.

Mike Riddle, the attending physician, was standing at the head of the bed. He looked at Robert and yelled, "I need two units of O negative blood STAT!" Then he looked at Christine and said, "Draw a CBC, FBP, PT, PTT, and lactic acid then take the fluids off the pump and run them wide open."

Christine opened the side panel of the pump and clicked the safety valve open to allow the fluids to infuse as fast as they could go into the vein.

Robert went to the phone and called the blood bank. He entered the order in the computer while Joyce Young the unit secretary went to the blood bank to pick it up.

Within five minutes, Robert had two units of blood in his hand. He handed the blood to Christine who was standing beside the patient's IV. She spiked the first bag with blood administering tubing. Then she connected it to the IV and opened it up. Then she spiked the second bag of blood with the other side of the blood administering tubing so both bags could infuse at the same time.

Dr. Riddle felt for a pulse and said, "He has a pulse, but it is weak."

Bert Summerland sat up and projectile vomited a missile of blood across the room, covering the white lab coat of one of the medical students.

The med student looked around the room in shock then slowly and carefully pulled his coat off and laid it on the floor.

"We have no pulse!" Dr. Riddle yelled, as he started chest compressions. Then he looked at Christine and asked, "Can you give the blood in any faster?"

"Not without a pressure cuff," she yelled.

"THEN GET A PRESSURE CUFF IN HERE," he yelled, as he pressed down on his patient's chest.

Robert ran to the storage room and found a pressure cuff. After making sure it worked, he charged back to the room and handed it to the coatless med student and told him to give it to Christine.

She took the cuff, slid a unit of blood through the sleeve, and began pumping it up. The more she pumped, the tighter the sleeve became which forced blood into the central line of the bleeding patient.

However, the more blood that was pumped into the patient, the more he bled. He was vomiting blood, had blood oozing from his ears, and had a constant stream dripping from his nose.

After about an hour of vigorous work, Dr. Riddle pronounced Bert Summerland dead. He had been given a total of four units of O negative blood, but had lost at least eight units of blood during the process.

The room looked like a massacre had taken place with blood covering the bed, the floor, and the walls.

After everyone left the room, Christine approached Carol Summerland and asked, "Will you give me a few minutes to clean the room a little before you go see your husband?"

"What?" Carol asked in shock. "Yes, I guess," she said and sank against the wall.

"Come sit in our conference room until the nurse is done with her work," Dennis Moon, the hospital chaplain said, as he took Mrs. Summerland by the arm and slowly led her to the conference room.

As they entered the room, he pulled a chair away from the table and helped her sit down. "Someone will come get us when the room is ready," he said, as he sat down in a chair beside her and took her hand.

Chapter 10

I took the elevator up to the third floor as soon as I heard about the death of Bert Summerland.

As I turned the corner and walked toward the nurses' station, I saw a group of people crowded together in deep discussion. The one leading the conversation was Mike Riddle, one of our attending physicians with what appeared to be residents and medical students listening intently.

Off to the right I saw a couple of nurses standing in front of a computer as they discussed something that they had pulled up on the screen.

When I got near the group, Dr. Riddle stopped talking and turned toward me. Then he looked at one of the residents and said, "Go check on the other patients."

"Hi, Dr. Riddle," I said, as I stuck my hand out.

He took my hand, shook it and said, "You sure were fast getting here."

"The sooner I can start the investigation the more likely it won't happen again," I said.

"If you find out what happened, let me know because I'm not sure myself," he said, as he scratched his head and added,

"Nothing in his health history would have caused this."

"What happened?"

"Let's go somewhere so we can talk privately," he said and began walking to the physicians lounge.

I followed without saying a word.

When we got to the lounge, he opened the door and held it for me to enter.

I went in and sat down in one of the chairs by the table.

He followed and sat down beside me.

After he got settled, he cleared his throat and said, "I've never seen anything like it before. It was like he hemorrhaged from the inside."

"What do you mean?"

"He was bleeding from his nose and ears," he said, as he unconsciously touched his nose with his index finger then continued, "And he vomited blood everywhere."

"Did he have a bleeding disorder?"

"He had kidney stones," he said in a loud voice and then repeated in a softer voice, "He only had kidney stones."

"Did he have any other history?"

"He had high blood pressure, gout, and restless legs, but nothing that would contribute to this."

"Was he taking any medications that could cause this?"

"No."

"Did you get any labs during the code?"

"Yes, I order the standard labs we get during a code."

"Was anything abnormal?"

"I haven't had a chance to check the labs," he said, as he rolled over toward the computer and signed onto his screen. "The patient died before the labs came back, and I've been busy with the death certificate."

I watched as he clicked onto the patient's name and

scrolled down until he reached the bar with labs written across the top in large black letters. He clicked on the labs bar and the screen instantly changed to light blue with a row of columns stretched out across the top. Running down the side was a list of labs that had been run from the patient's blood while he had been in the hospital.

Dr. Riddle pointed to the first column and said, "This is the labs that were run during the code."

"Is anything unusual?" I asked, as I moved closer to the computer screen.

"His BUN and Creatinine were a little elevated, his PCV was 21 and HGB was 6.8 which were indicative of him losing the amount of blood he had lost," he said, as he took a deep breath and exclaimed, "Oh my God, this is the problem! His PTT was 327. His blood was no thicker than water."

"Was he on prophylactic heparin?"

"No, he was ambulating around the halls several times a day, and I didn't see a need for heparin," he said, as he clicked off his screen. "And prophylactic heparin wouldn't cause someone's PTT to be that high.

"I understand that," I said, "But what would?"

"I have no idea," he said, "Maybe liver disease, but his liver was fine."

I looked across the empty room as I tried to think of what may have caused the patient's PTT to be so high. After several seconds, I asked, "Did you ask his wife if she wanted an autopsy?"

"Yes, I told her that it would be best to have an autopsy so we could find out what happened and she agreed."

"That's great," I said, "Thanks for getting her to agree to have the autopsy done."

"Well, it's the only way we'll know what really happened."

"That's true," I said, as I got up and walked to the door. "Thanks for your time," I said and I walked out the door.

I went to the nurses' desk and stood for a few seconds looking at everyone as they scrambled around trying to look busy. I looked at each person to observe how they reacted to the death.

When they noticed me standing there, everyone stopped talking, turned and looked at me.

Then a lady in her late forties smiled and asked, "Can I help you?"

"My name is Ted Maxwell," I said, as I stuck my hand out. "I'm in charge of patient safety in the hospital."

She smiled, but didn't shake my hand. Then she looked at my name tag and asked without expression, "What can I do for you Ted?"

"I need to speak to the nurse that had Mr. Summerland."

"Let's see," she said and looked at the assignment board. "That would be Christine Eaton."

"Do you know where I might find her?"

"I'm right here," said a voice from behind me.

I turned around and found the lady that was sitting at the computer when I came to the floor. She forced a smile, took a deep breath, and slowly let it out. Then she asked, "What can I do for you?"

"I talked to Dr. Riddle and he told me what happened to Mr. Summerland, but I'd like your point of view," I said, as I looked at a couple of chairs in the back of the nurses' station. I pointed at them and asked, "Can we sit back there?"

"Sure," she said and started walking toward the chairs.

She sat in the first chair she came to and I went to the second and sat down. I laid my notepad beside the computer and smiled trying to project a calming and nonthreatening atmosphere.

She smiled back.

"What can you tell me about the patient's death?" I asked, as I reached for my notepad.

"What do you want to know?" she asked with irritation in her voice. "I paged the resident twice before he responded and then his response was to tell me that they were rounding and would see the patient when they got to the room."

"Did you explain that the patient was bleeding?"

"At that time he was bleeding from his nose and ears and the resident said to have him hold pressure on his nose until they could see him."

"Do you think the resident's delay caused the patient to die?"

"I have no idea," she said, "But it certainly wouldn't have hurt for him to look in on the patient when I asked him to."

I wrote on my notepad that the resident didn't respond to nurse's concerns, before I asked, "Was the patient given any blood thinner?"

"I didn't give him any," she said, "He was up ambulating and had a compression hose on to help prevent blood clots, so I think he was covered pretty well."

"We're going to do an autopsy on him so make sure you leave everything in place," I said, as I closed my notepad. "I want you to send whatever IV fluids he had infusing and the tubing with him when you send him to the morgue."

"Do you want the IV pump sent with the patient or just the fluids and tubing?"

"I don't think we need the pump," I said. "The fluids and tubing--------should be all we need."

"Alright, I'll take them off the pump when we wrap the body."

"Sounds good," I said, as I stood up. "If you think of anything that might be important please give me a call," and I handed her my card.

She took my card, looked at it and said, "I'll call you if I think of anything," then slipped it in her pocket.

"Thanks for your time," I said and I walked around the desk. I took one more look around the nurses' station then I walked away.

When I got to the elevator, I pulled my cell phone out and called one of my best friends, Detective Mark Stone with the Westbrook Police Department, and told him of the situation.

"Why didn't you call me after the first death?" he asked in a stern voice.

"Because I thought it was an accident, and I could handle it internally, but with two patients dying from what appears to be an overdose I decided I needed to get you involved."

"Do you have proof that the second victim was killed by an overdose?"

"Not yet. Doctor Bennett is going to perform an autopsy on him."

"Don't move the body until I can come by and see if I can gather some evidence."

"It's too late. They just rolled it toward the morgue."

"That's just great," Mark said with irritation in his voice. "If it turns out that this patient was overdosed and the killer left some evidence, then it's all contaminated."

"It would have been contaminated anyway because of everybody working the code."

"If I found something, I could have ruled out the people working the code as potential suspects."

"I'm sorry. I didn't think about you wanting to look for evidence."

After a deep pause Mark asked, "When should you get the results of the autopsy?"

"I'm supposed to meet with Doctor Bennett in the morning at about eight o'clock so he can tell me the results."

"I'll see you then and we can discuss this further," he said and my phone went dead.

I closed my phone, put it in my pocket, and went home.

Chapter 11

The next morning I was sitting at my desk entering the information I had gathered into my database when I heard a knock at the door. I hit the save button and closed the screen. Then I looked toward the door and said, "Come in."

Mark Stone opened the door and asked, "Am I too early?" as he looked around the room and sat down in one of the chairs.

He was wearing a pair of navy blue Wrangler jeans, light blue button down shirt, and a black leather jacket to cover his Glock 9mm that was attached to his shoulder holster. His boots were eastern rattlesnake with two inch heals which made his six foot four inch, two hundred and sixty pound muscular frame look even more intimidating.

"No, Doctor Bennett should be here any minute," I answered.

"I didn't mean to be short with you last night, but whenever you have a suspicious death and you call the police, you need to leave everything in the room undisturbed," Mark said as he pulled the chair closer to my desk.

"I know that now," I said, "I guess I wasn't thinking."

"There's nothing we can do about it now," he said, "And anyway, at this point we're not even sure it was a murder."

"That's true," I said as someone tapped lightly on the door.

"Come in," I yelled.

Dr. Garland Bennett opened the door and glanced at Mark before asking, "Do you have time to go over the autopsy report?"

"Sure, I'll take time," I said, as I pointed to one of the chairs and said, "Have a seat."

He stood at the door without moving.

"Garland this is Mark Stone with the police department," I said as a way of introduction. "I asked him to be here today."

"That might be a good thing," Doctor Bennett said as he stepped inside my office and closed the door.

Then he sat down and started shaking his head. "These things that are going on inside the hospital have really got me puzzled," he said and he opened the manila envelope he had in his hand.

"What are you talking about?"

"One patient died from extremely high potassium, and this guy died with a PTT greater than 300."

"Are you saying they are connected?" I asked with concern.

"No, that's not what I'm saying," he said assuredly. "I'm just saying that it is odd that two people died the way they did."

"Well, what did you find when you did the autopsy on Mr. Summerland?"

Dr. Bennett opened the manila envelope and glanced at the report. He lifted the top sheet of paper and said, "He did have kidney stones, but that had nothing to do with his death."

"How did he die?"

"As I said before, his PTT was greater than 300 which led to internal bleeding from an ulcer he had on the lining of his abdomen, he had seeping from esophageal erosion which contributed to his blood loss when he had projectile vomiting. He also had small broken vessels in his nose and some bleeding in his brain as blood began to seep through the vessels."

"How did his PTT get so high?"

"I looked at his liver to see if there was any cirrhosis, but the liver was in perfect condition. I looked at his pancreas, gallbladder, and bile ducts and I found no abnormality," he said, as he scratched his head. "The only conclusion I could come up with was that it was medically induced, so I took the bag of IV fluid that was hanging and analyzed it."

"He had normal saline infusing."

"Wait, let me finish," he said. "As I began looking at the bag, I noticed a small puncture in the port where additives are inserted. So, I took a sample of the fluid and sent it to the lab to be analyzed."

"Have you got the results back from the lab?"

"I got the results just before I came to talk to you," he said. "The bag of fluid was filled with heparin. The sample I sent to the lab indicated that the fluid in the bag had ten times more heparin than in a premixed bag of heparin."

"Did someone on 3N put heparin in the bag, or was it in the bag when the fluid was delivered to the floor?" I asked, as I propped my elbows on my desk.

"Do they have access to that strength of heparin on the floor?"

"No, they don't have access to that type of heparin on any

of the floors," I said, "But could someone have brought it from home."

"Anything is possible," he said. "But I'm more inclined to believe that it was in the fluid when it was brought to the floor."

"So, do you think someone targeted this patient, or was it a random killing by putting heparin in the IV fluid?" Mark asked.

"I'm not sure if they targeted the patient or not, but I do know that the patient was killed by a heparin overdose and his bag of fluid had an extremely high level in it," Doctor Bennett answered.

"If that is the case, we need to pull all the IV fluid they have on the floor and check each bag," I said, as I stood up and walked toward the door.

"Where are you going?" Doctor Bennett asked.

"I don't have time to wait," I said, "I need to check the bags of fluid that are on the floor," and I walked out the door and rushed to the stairs.

"I'll go with you," Mark yelled as he ran after me.

I ran up the stairs taking two at a time until I was at the door announcing the entrance to the third floor. I went straight to Julie Wells, the nurse manager for 3N, and stated, "I need the nurses to stop all the IV fluids that they have infusing immediately."

"What? Stop all the fluids?" she asked, as she looked at me as if I had lost my mind.

"Yes, stop the fluids."

"Why?"

"I'll explain later," I said, "Just get everything stopped."

"Alright, if you say so," she said, as she walked to the nurses' desk and started calling everyone together.

"I need to look at all the fluids you have in your supply room," I said, as I started down the hall.

"I need a copy of the autopsy report," Mark said when we reached the door to the supply room.

"I'll get Doctor Bennett to fax a copy to you when we get back to my office," I said and reached for the door knob.

I opened the door to the supply room and started looking for the bay that contained IV fluids. I found them positioned in the middle rack between the suction equipment and Foley catheter kits.

As I pulled the first container of fluid off the shelf, Julie walked in the supply room and asked, "What is this all about?"

"The bag of fluid that was hanging in Mr. Summerland's room had heparin injected in it and I don't know if that was the only bag or if there are more bags with heparin added to them."

"Oh my God!" she exclaimed. "Are you saying Mr. Summerland was murdered?"

"That's what it looks like."

She picked up a bag and asked, "Can you tell if the bags have heparin in them or not?" and held one up in front of her eyes.

"Dr. Bennett saw where heparin had been injected into the bag but to tell you the truth, the only way to really know is to have them analyzed."

"Then take them away," she ordered. "I want all the bags of fluid removed from my supply room."

"I think we should also analyze the bags that were hanging in the patients' rooms," I said, as I pulled a container filled with sterile cups off the shelf. "We can get samples out of each bag and label them with the patients name and room number."

"I'll let my nurses know," she said and she walked out the door carrying the sterile cups.

After looking through a couple of storage rooms, I found a cart and Mark and I began stacking the containers of fluid on the cart. When it was filled, I stacked the remaining bags of fluid on the floor around the cart and backed up against the counter to wait for someone from the lab to arrive to help transport the bags.

After several minutes, the door opened and Dewayne Barker, supervisor for the hospital lab, walked in pushing a cart to help transport the fluid.

He looked at the pile on the floor and said, "That's a lot to be tested."

"There's more," I said, "I have the nurses getting samples from all the bags that are hanging in the patients' rooms."

"I may be here a while," Dewayne said, "But I'll run the samples myself before I leave tonight."

"Let's get the fluid down to the lab so you can get started," I said and opened the door.

Dewayne followed me out the door pushing his cart filled with bags of fluid. We stopped at the nurses' station and picked up the containers of fluid that had been removed from the patients' rooms.

After everything was gathered, we took the samples to the lab.

I parked the cart by the door and said, "I'll be in my office waiting for the results of your tests."

"It might take a while."

"Just call me with the results," I said and walked away.

"I need to get back to the police station," Mark said as we were leaving.

"Thanks for coming," I said, "I'll get a copy of the autopsy to you as fast as I can."

"Send me a copy of the lab results and see if you can get a copy of the autopsy report of the other patient that you were talking about faxed over, too," Mark said. "I'd like to have both on hand to compare findings."

"I'll see what I can do."

"I need all the information I can get," Mark said, and he walked away.

Chapter 12

I turned to go to my office, but changed directions and went to the elevator as I decided to go to the supply warehouse and ask to speak to the person that delivered supplies to 3N. Even though it was a long shot, I wanted to ask anyone that might have information about the bag of fluid that contained heparin.

The elevator door opened and I walked inside. I looked at the panel, found the button with a large B and mashed it with my thumb. Within a few seconds, I was on my way to the basement.

As I got off the elevator, I could heard the distant screeching sound of the conveyer as it automatically turned on and off while delivering large baskets of linen to the laundry room to be cleaned.

The floor was concrete with patches of hunter green from the remains of an old paint job that had been scraped away from years of wear and a long time of neglect. I turned right and slowly walked toward the distant sound. When I got near the corner, I looked up at the ceiling where two large rusty steel rails were bolted side by side along with oil covered steel chains attached to cogs to move the conveyer when it powered on.

As I started to take a step, I jumped and turned to my right when I heard what sounded like feet shuffling in the shadowy corner behind a stack of empty laundry baskets that were waiting to be picked up by the conveyer belt. I looked in that direction for several seconds without moving to see if I could determine what I had heard. When I didn't hear anything else, I decided it was my imagination, so I continued walking toward the supply warehouse.

As I walked I stayed clear of the conveyer belts and kept in mind that there were several areas where people could hide because of the dark due to low lighting along the path. Several lights were out because of burnt out bulbs and the neglect of the hospital to keep the area maintained.

I quickened my pace when I saw the door to the supply warehouse. When I got near, I took my badge out of my pocket and scanned the pass key to open the lock.

After I heard the click of the lock, I turned the knob and walked inside the warehouse. It was an open room with pallets stacked everywhere. I saw gray shelves in the back with individual supplies separated by codes.

As I got close to the counter, a man dressed in dark blue coveralls stepped toward me and asked, "What can I do for you?"

"My name is Ted Maxwell with patient safety," I said and showed him my badge.

"Mr. Ted, how can I help you?" the man asked.

"I need to talk to the person that delivered supplies to 3N yesterday."

"What did he do?"

"I just need to ask him a few questions."

"Give me a minute," he said, "I'll need to look at my log," and he walked behind the counter.

He pulled out a ledger and opened it. After turning several sheets of paper, he brought his finger down the last page and said, "Leo Brown delivered supplies to 3N yesterday."

"Is Leo here today?"

"I think he's in the back loading his cart for today," the man said. "I'll go check," and he walked to the back of the warehouse.

I stood at the counter and watched as people walked from the back carrying large boxes of hospital supplies that were probably not floor stock and placing them on carts that were brought down by unit secretaries. After the secretary checked to make sure everything that they had ordered was in the box, they rolled the carts away and disappeared in the darkness of the basement.

After several minutes of waiting, a man in his early twenties walked up to me and said, "I'm Leo Brown. I hear you want to talk to me."

"Oh, hi Leo," I said trying to maintain a friendly atmosphere. "Did you deliver supplies to 3N yesterday?"

"Yes, I delivered to 3N yesterday," he said. "Why?"

"Did you notice anything unusual with your delivery?"

"Not that I can remember," he said. "Why?"

"Did you see anyone at your cart before you took the supplies to the floor?"

"No, I didn't see anybody," he said then demanded, "What's this all about?"

"Some of the supplies were tampered with, and I'm trying to decide who tampered with them."

"I just delivered the supplies," he said defensively. "I didn't do anything to them."

"And you saw no one around your cart."

"No, I didn't see anyone around my cart, but now that you mention it there was an extra box of IV fluid on my cart."

"What did you do with it?"

"Put it up with the rest of the fluid," he said. "I didn't want to bring it back down here, and we've probably shorted them in the past so I thought it would equal out."

"Do you remember what kind of fluid it was?"

"It was 1000 ml bags of fluid, but I don't remember which bags it was."

"How could you tell which ones were extra?"

"Because all the other boxes were sealed and this box was open."

"Was the extra box full or just partly filled?"

"I remember it was a full box because I was thinking that it was odd that it was open."

"But you don't remember what type of fluid it was?"

"It might have been normal saline, but I really don't remember."

I looked at a large pallet filled with boxes of IV fluid as I tried to think of something else to ask, but nothing came to mind. There really wasn't enough evidence to prompt any questions and this guy looked like he really didn't know anything so I decided it was time to go.

"Thanks for talking to me," I said, as I handed him my card. "If you think of anything else please call me."

"Am I in trouble?" he asked, as he took my card.

"Not as far as I'm concerned," I said, as I smiled. "Please call me if you think of anything else.'

"I will," he said, as he put my card in his shirt pocket and hurried to the back.

I looked around at the massive warehouse, then turned

and walked out the door. I slowly walked down the corridor to the elevator and went to my office.

Chapter 13

When I reached my office, I saw Hanna Johns, Westbrook Medical Center's Chief Nursing Officer, pacing back and forth in front of my door with her arms crossed. She stopped pacing and stared at me as I approached.

She was hired three years ago to consolidate the work force and increase profits. Bringing ideas from other hospitals in which she had worked, she promised to increase productivity from the nurses and decrease the need for ancillary help such as nursing assistance and secretaries, but with an increase in un-paying customers her goals were far from being reached. As each day passed and the hospital's revenue continuing to decline, she saw her job in jeopardy.

"Where have you been?" she demanded, as she took a step toward me.

"I was in the supply warehouse talking to the person that delivered supplies to 3N yesterday," I said in a calm voice.

"I've been waiting on you for twenty minutes," she said, as she tried to hide her irritation.

"Part of my job requires me to go throughout the hospital and talk to potential witnesses when a patient dies," I said.

"That means that I'm not in my office a lot of the time."

"I'm sorry," she said, as she tried to smile. "I didn't mean to sound angry."

"Is there a problem?"

She looked up and down the hall without saying anything. Then she stepped a little closer and whispered, "I'd rather talk in your office."

"Sure, we can talk in my office," I said, as I walked to my door and unlocked it.

I held it open as she walked inside and sat down in the first chair she came to. Then I closed the door and sat in the chair behind my desk. I put my arms on my desktop, leaned a little forward and asked, "What do you want to talk about?"

She cleared her throat and said, "It has come to my attention that two patients have died under questionable conditions."

"Yes, that is true," I said. "That is one of the reasons I was at the supply warehouse earlier."

"Have you discovered how they died?"

"The first patient, Mrs. Moore died from an overdose of potassium and the second patient, Mr. Summerland, died from an overdose of heparin." I said as I tried to decide whether to tell her about another potential incident, but then I continued, "We also had a patient in the ICU that had an unexpected drop in his blood pressure. The nurses contributed it to his nitroglycerine drip, but with these other deaths I'm concerned his drip might have been tampered with."

"Did the patient die?"

"No. They caught it in time to correct his blood pressure by giving him several boluses of fluid."

"What's the patient's name?"

"John Moss."

"I can understand how someone can get to much nitroglycerine, but how can a patient get too much heparin and potassium?" she said with surprise. "We regulate both of those medications very strictly."

"That's what has me puzzled," I said, "Pharmacy is the only one with access to those drugs. At least in the concentration that had to be used to overdose both victims the way they were."

"Have you questioned the people in pharmacy?"

"Not yet," I said. "I'm still looking into a couple of things to try to determine exactly how Mr. Summerland died."

"Do you think it was accidental or intentional?"

"I'm not sure."

"This is a very delicate situation, and the way you handle it could make a lot of difference in how the hospital looks."

"What do you mean?"

"I need you to handle the investigation as discreetly as possible."

"That's my intention," I said, "But I need to question everyone involved."

"I know you do," she said and stood up. "I just hope this don't get out to the public."

"If it does, it won't be because I said anything," I said, as I stood up and walked to the door.

"I don't want you to get the wrong idea," she said. "I care deeply about our patients and their safety."

"But you'd like the reputation of the hospital to stay intact," I said, as I opened the door.

"Yes, I would," she said and she walked out of my office.

I watched in disbelief at what I had just heard as she walked down the hall. After she rounded the corner, I closed the door and sat down at my desk to wait for the lab results from the bags of fluid.

Chapter 14

I leaned back in my chair and began running ideas through my mind as to why anyone would want to harm patients in the hospital. They were already at a disadvantage because they were sick or, in Mr. Summerland's case, in a lot of pain, so what would be the purpose.

Did someone have a grudge against the hospital? Had someone been reprimanded and wanted to get revenge?

As I was pondering these questions, I heard a soft knock on the door.

I turned toward the door and said, "Come in."

The door opened and Dewayne Barker stepped inside looking exhausted from long hours of running tests. After a sigh, he announced, "I have the test results," and he held a stack of paper in the air.

"Come in and sit down," I said, as I pointed to a chair in front of my desk.

He closed the door.

"I brought you a report from each sample to keep in your file," he said, as he went to the chair and sat down.

"Thanks," I said.

"Here it is," he said and he laid a stack of papers on my desk. "I also have a summary of the test results and I thought we'd go over it while I'm here."

"Great," I said. "What did you find?"

"I found three bags of fluid that were in the supply room with heparin injected into them," he said. "They were all bags of normal saline and had the same equivalent that was given to Mr. Summerland. There was ten times the normal rate of heparin to normal saline."

"Could you tell that the bags were tampered with before you tested them?"

"I could, but only because I was looking for a puncture site," he said. "The person that injected the heparin into the bags of fluid used a very small needle and they shifted the outer bag around so the puncture site was along the seam."

"So, if you didn't suspect that something had been injected into the bag you'd never notice it."

"No, you'd never see it."

"What about the samples taken from the patients rooms?"

"Two samples tested positive for heparin," he said. "One was from room 338 and the other was from room 326."

"Did they write the patients' names on the samples?"

"Oh, I'm sorry," he said. "According to the bottles, the patient in room 338 is Brad Hicks, and the patient in room 326 is Ray Elmore."

I picked up my phone and called 3N. It rang several times before a female answered the phone and said, "3N," and then she asked, "How can I help you?"

"This is Ted Maxwell," I said, "I need to speak to the nurse that has Brad Hicks in room 338 and Ray Elmore in room 326."

"Just a minute please," she said and I was put on hold.

I waited what seemed like an hour, but according to my phone it was only four minutes and forty eight seconds before a male voice came on the line and announced, "Robert speaking," and then he asked, "How can I help you."

"Do you have the patient in room 338 or 326?"

"Who is this?"

"I'm sorry," I said, "This is Ted Maxwell."

"I have 338," he said, "Why?"

"The fluid that he had hanging in his room had heparin in it," I said, "I need you to draw a PTT and send it to the lab STAT."

"Do you want me to do anything else?"

"Don't let him get out of bed until you have the results from the lab."

"Alright," he said.

"Can I speak to the person that has room 326?"

"Sure, just a minute," he said and again I was put on hold.

This time I only waited three minutes before a lady picked up and said, "This is Christine," and then she asked, "How can I help you?"

"Christine, this is Ted Maxwell," I said, "I need you to draw a PTT on the patient in room 326 and send it to the lab STAT."

"Oh no!" she exclaimed. "Not again."

"Calm down," I said, "This is just precautionary."

"Alright, I'll send it right now," she said, as she put the phone down on the receiver.

I put my phone down, leaned back and said, "Now we wait."

"I think I'll go to the lab and wait for the samples," Dewayne said, as he got up and started walking toward the door. "I don't want any delays with the results," and he walked out of my office, closing the door behind him.

I picked up my phone and punched in the number to the pharmacy responsible for covering 3N. After the third ring, the phone was answered and a female voice said, "3N pharmacy," and she asked, "How can I help you?"

"Can I speak to a pharmacist please?" I asked.

"Who may I say is calling?" she said.

"This is Ted Maxwell with patient safety."

Within seconds, a male voice said, "This is Walter," and he asked, "What can I do for you?"

"My name is Ted Maxwell with patient safety," I said, "We've had an issue with patients getting overdosed on heparin, and I was wondering if you had a bottle of protamine sulfate available in your pharmacy."

"We normally don't keep that up here," he said, "It's a very risky medication to administer and requires strict monitoring."

"I understand, but if you had an emergency, how quickly could you get it to the floor."

"It comes from central pharmacy," he said. "I guess I could send someone to get it which would take about ten minutes."

"If we had someone bleeding because of a heparin overdose we wouldn't have ten minutes."

"Are you anticipating a heparin overdose?"

"We've already had one today, and we have two patients that we're running STAT PTT's on as we speak," I said, "It's very likely that we may need to use the drug to reverse the effects of heparin."

"I'll order a bottle and have someone run to central pharmacy to get it so we'll have it just in case."

"Thanks," I said, "I should know something within the

next thirty minutes."

"I'll have the protamine sulfate if we need it," he said and hung up the phone.

I put the phone down and leaned back to wait for the results of the STAT labs.

Ten minutes after I arranged to have the protamine sulfate ready on 3N, Dewayne Barker with the hospital lab called to let me know that their PTT's were elevated, but neither was dangerously high.

After getting the news from Dewayne, I called Walter Key, the pharmacist on 3N and let him know that I didn't need the protamine sulfate today. He seemed a little perturbed that he had ordered something that wouldn't be used, but he acknowledged that he was thankful that the patients wouldn't be subjected to protamine sulfate treatment.

I thanked him for his effort and hung up the phone. Then I locked my filing cabinet and went home.

Chapter 15

Larry Adcock, Chief Financial Officer and CEO of Westbrook Medical Center, was standing in front of the directors of each department of the hospital at the annual business meeting, addressing the current financial circumstances of the hospital. He pointed to a graph that was projected upon the wall and said, "As you can see, we have an increasing deficit in our profit because of the amount of patients that are admitted without insurance. They have, up to this point, been given no different treatment than our other patients, with one big exception. Our doctors tend to run more tests on them than they do the patients with insurance."

The projector changed to another chart, which represented hospital stay. He pointed to the chart and said, "On the side I have numbers which represent days in the hospital, and at the top you'll see the average stay. The first column represents patients with insurance and the second column represents patients without insurance. As you can see, patients without insurance stay an average of three days longer than patients with insurance."

He pointed to a column in blue and said, "Both of these

patients had pneumonia, but one stayed two days longer than the other one. Can you tell me which one stayed two days?"

All the directors looked down at a sheet of paper in front of them at the same time without answering the question.

"It seems obvious that we are treating people that are not paying us better than our paying customers," he said, as he laid his pointer on the table. "I understand we have to answer to the insurance companies, but everyone should be treated the same."

After turning the projector off, he pulled his chair out and sat down. He looked around the table and added, "This document leads me to believe that we are better off without insurance and this can't be true. I want each of you to devise a plan to decrease the hospital stay of patients without insurance and present a power point next week outlining your plan. Give me projected numbers and documentation to back the numbers up."

He took one long look around the table without smiling and said, "At this rate our hospital will be operating in the red within the next month."

Then he stood up, glared at each director and said, "If this trend doesn't change and we don't start making a profit, some of you may find yourselves out of a job," and he walked out of the room.

After the door closed, everyone sat looking at each other for several minutes without saying a word. Then Hanna Johns stood up and said, "Alright, you've heard what the man said. We've got to start getting patients out of the hospital faster."

"He didn't say get patients out faster," Tony Boswell, director over rehab services said. "He said that we needed to get patients without insurance out faster."

"That's a doctor thing," Hanna said, as she glanced at

Doctor Willie Pike the Chief of Staff.

"I'll meet with my doctors tomorrow and have them speed up the discharge process," Dr. Pike said, as he looked at Hanna and added, "It would be helpful if the nurses looked at the patients' information and let the doctors know which patient had insurance or not."

"We have people hired to do that," she responded. "The doctors just need to listen to them when they tell them the patient needs to be discharged."

"I don't see the point in discharging patients when they just turn around and come back to the hospital," Tony said.

"I see your point," Hanna Johns said and looked around the room. "Maybe we can come up with a plan that we can implement to help prevent them from coming back to the hospital."

"Maybe we could transfer the patients without insurance to a charity hospital once they are stable," Brian Dawson, Director of Surgery said.

"If we did that, someone would sue us for discrimination," Hanna said then reiterated, "We just need to find a way to keep them from being readmitted into the hospital."

"Isn't that what the person did that killed those patients on 3N?" Tony said.

"No, that person just randomly overdosed patients," she said. "One of the patients he killed had insurance and the other one didn't."

"Too bad he didn't just target the patients without insurance," Tony said with a laugh.

"Remember, we're in this business to help people," Hanna scolded.

"Maybe so," Tony said, as he stood up and added, "But we're not a charity hospital."

"No, we're not but we can't turn people away."

"I know," he said, "I'm just tired and ready to go home."

"It's been a long day," Hanna said, "Let's go home and think about how we can solve this problem."

Everyone stood up and slowly walked out of the meeting room. They agreed to go home and try to come up with a plan to help save the hospital.

Chapter 16

I got to work at eight o'clock the following morning and went straight to 3N to check on the patients that had been given the fluid with heparin added.

When I got to the floor, I looked at the board to see which nurse was assigned to the patients I needed to see so I could ask to speak to the nurse by name. Christine, with whom I'd spoken yesterday, was the nurse for the patient in room 326. Virgil Edge, who is normally in charge, had the patient in room 338.

Christine noticed me as I walked to the nurses' station. She got up and walked toward me before I could ask to see her. When she got near she asked, "Did you come to see me?"

"Actually, I came to check on the patients that had heparin yesterday," I said, as I moved closer and asked, "How's the patient in room 326 doing today?"

"Oh, he's doing fine," she said, "In fact, he's going home today."

"Really, that's great," I said.

"Yes, I was a little surprised because it seemed like he was pretty sick yesterday," she said, "It just goes to show that I never know what the doctors are thinking."

"Do you think he's too sick to go home?"

"I'm not sure," she said, "They put him on PO antibiotics and said he could finish his recovering at home."

"When do you think he'll be leaving?"

"I'm waiting on the social worker," she said, "She's going to have to get the medicine for him because he can't afford to buy it himself."

"So, once he gets his medicine he'll be discharged."

"Yes, I have the discharge order all ready," she said, "I'm just waiting on the social worker."

"I would like to speak to Virgil for a minute," I said, as I looked around to see if I could find him behind the nurses' station. "Do you know where he might be?"

She looked at the clock, then said, "He might be in the med room," and added, "I'll go see if I can find him," and she walked away.

I stood with my elbow leaning against the counter as I watched for Virgil to approach. I spotted him before he saw me as he rounded the corner and walked up the hall toward the nurses' station. He kept his head down as he walked and appeared to be in deep thought.

"Virgil, can I speak to you a minute?" I asked, as he started to walk past.

"What?" he asked, as he looked toward me.

"Can I talk to you a minute?" I asked.

"Oh, hey, Ted," he said when he recognized me. He moved closer and asked, "Is anything wrong?"

"I'm just checking on the patients from yesterday," I said.

"Alright, what do you want to know?"

"How's the guy in 338 doing today?"

"He's doing great."

"Did he have any problems throughout the night?"

"No, in fact he's going home this morning," he said.

"That's odd," I said, "So is the guy in room 326."

"The doctors came up and said they were going to discharge as many as they could this morning. Then they started writing discharge orders as soon as they finished rounding."

"That's good we can empty rooms for new patients that need to be admitted," I said with enthusiasm.

"I guess if you say so," he said solemnly.

"What's wrong?" I asked. "Do you not think the patient is ready to go home?"

"Most of these patients are non-compliant with their medicines and they'll be back in a couple of weeks."

"You have no control over what the patients do when they are at home," I said, "Your job is to do the best you can while they're in the hospital, to get them better and then send them home."

"I know," he said and he walked away.

I watched him for a few seconds, then turned and walked toward the elevator. When the door opened, I got on and went to my office to work on a presentation I was going to present at a safety conference in a couple of weeks.

As I worked on the presentation, I continued thinking about the two mysterious deaths on 3N and wondered who could be responsible. Were they connected? Did the same individual contribute to the patients' deaths? What was the motive?

I got my notepad out of my desk drawer and scanned over the information I had gathered on the deaths. As I read over my notes, I determined that I had nothing to connect the two patients together. So, I put my pad away and closed the drawer.

After taking my glasses off, I rubbed my eyes in an attempt to rub the tiredness away. Then I turned back to my computer and started working on the presentation again. My mind slowly began to wander again.

I looked at the clock, which indicated that it was 3:15 in the afternoon, so I saved the work I had done and turned my computer off. Then I got up, locked the filing cabinet and went home.

Chapter 17

The Executioner had scouted throughout the hospital and found his next victim on the medical intensive care unit located on the fourth floor. Dressed as a member of housekeeping, he was mopping floors, moving down the hall, going into rooms as would be expected. He glanced periodically to see if anyone was paying attention to him. It was as if he was invisible, no one noticed him.

When he got to the target's room, he slipped in; checking to make sure the nurse wasn't inside.

He placed the mop near the bed and moved to the head of the bed.

He looked at the man in his early sixties with pneumonia who would probably recover after several weeks of aggressive therapy. He had no insurance and he was costing the hospital thousands of dollars every day that he remained in the hospital on a ventilator. This was his second admission in six months with the same diagnosis. Unless he changed his lifestyle, he would be back several more times in the coming years.

The Executioner was told that the hospital couldn't afford

to keep admitting the uninsured. It was his job to help eliminate the potential risk of this happening.

The target was frail, with a tube protruding out of his mouth taped to his face and secured with tape around his head. That tube was attached to a larger tube that was connected to a ventilator. Several lights flashed on the machine as it did the work of breathing for the man. When the man moved, an alarm sounded periodically from the massive machine.

The Executioner froze and listened for footsteps coming down the hall, waiting to see if the nurse would come to check on the patient.

When no one came into the room, he quickly got to work. He was pleased to note that his target's hands were tied to the side of the bed, which would make his job much easier.

Keeping an eye on the door, the mysterious figure leaned over the target and took out his pocket knife. He cut the tape holding the ventilating tube in place and pulled the tube out.

He watched as the target's eyes flew open, with his body stiffening in an attempt to breathe. As the patient struggled for breath, the Executioner placed the cardiac leads and pulse oximeter on himself to keep the monitor from alarming.

The Executioner placed a pillow over the target's face to speed up the process, as the patient struggled against his restraints.

When the target quit struggling, the Executioner quickly replaced the pillow. Then moved the cardiac leads and pulse oximeter back on the patient, picked up his mop, and moved on down the hall.

Chapter 18

Henry Alexander was sitting at the desk charting his assessment and periodically glancing at the monitor. The monitor had alarmed every few minutes since he came on shift. Henry had checked on the patient several times and even changed the leads, but it continued to alarm. He was behind in his charting because he had checked on the patient so often. He was just finishing his charting of vital signs taken over the last two hours and was about to chart intake and output when the monitor alarmed again.

He looked at Susan Brunner who was at a computer beside him and said, "I think we need a new monitor for Mr. Sims. This one isn't working right."

"He may have pulled his leads off."

"I've got his hands tied against the bedrail," he said. "I don't see how he could reach it."

"Just because you have him restrained doesn't mean he can't get the leads off."

Henry responded, "He is too weak to pull a Houdini."

"Then maybe you should go check on him," she said, as she started to get up.

"He was fine thirty minutes ago, and I've been in his room all night," he protested. "I'm way behind on my charting."

"Anything can happen in thirty minutes," she said, as she started walking toward his room. "And charting can wait."

"Wait a minute, I'm coming," he grumbled, as he started to get up. "He's my patient. I'll go check on him, even if I don't think anything is wrong," he mumbled, as he walked around the desk and went toward his patient's room.

"Since I'm up, I'll go with you anyway, just in case you need me," she said and she walked with him down the hall.

When Henry opened the door and walked past the curtain, he flipped the light on and yelled, "CRAP! He's pulled his tube out!" and he ran to the head of the bed, grabbed the ambu bag and started bagging him.

Susan looked at the monitor, which showed a flat line. She ran to the patient and felt for a pulse and said, "No pulse," then she flattened the bed and started chest compressions.

Henry hit the code button, which alerted everyone on the floor of the situation. He then looked down at the tube lying on the floor and asked, "How could he pull out his tube, his hands were tied?"

"Where there's a will there's a way," Susan mumbled as she continued with compressions.

Sonya McGee rushed through the door, shortly followed by respiratory and pharmacy. "What happened?" she demanded as she moved beside Susan and added, "I'll take over with chest compressions. You go get the crash cart."

"When we came to check on him, his ET tube was lying on the floor, no pulse, no respirations," Henry said.

"Who is he, and what's his history?" Dr. McGee asked.

"His name is Rick Sims. He came in septic with pneumonia two weeks ago," Henry said. "He has been on a ventilator since."

"He has been on a ventilator for two weeks?" she asked.

"Yes, he has."

"Susan, draw some labs," Dr. McGee said, "I want you to get a FBP, CBC, PTT, and a blood gas."

Susan ran and got some collection tubes. Then moved the IV pump to the side and reached over to the patient's central line, sticking out of the left side of his neck. After pulling a syringe of blood and discarding it, she started pulling blood for the labs. She carefully filled each collection tube to the desired level and labeled them with the patient's name. She then took a blood gas from the arterial line in the patient's left wrist, labeled it with the patient's name, and carried it to the desk to be sent to the lab.

After placing the tubes of blood in a bio-hazardous bag, she pulled lab slips and sent the blood to the lab. Then she went back in the room to be ready to assist with whatever she needed to do.

When she walked through the door, Susan noticed that Dr. Lynn Dutton had arrived and was performing chest compressions. Dr. McGee was watching the monitor for any signs of a heart beat while the respiratory therapist was at the head of the bed giving breathes. Bill Franks was pushing an amp of bicarbonate through the patient's central line.

"Does anyone need to be relieved?" Susan asked.

"I'm fine," Dr. Dutton said, "Just check on the labs, and let me know what they are when you get them."

"Sure," Susan said, as she walked out of the room and went to the desk to be ready to take the blood gas report when the lab called with the results.

Within five minutes, the lab called with the results on the blood gas. Susan wrote it down. Then went to the room and handed it to Dr. McGee who was still standing at the foot of the bed watching the monitor.

Dr. McGee looked at the blood gas results and asked, "How many amps of bicarb have we given him?"

"Two," Dr. Dutton said, "I know he has to be in metabolic acidosis."

"His PH is 7.21, HCO3 is 20, PaO2 is 68, SaO2 is 68," Dr. McGee said.

"How long have we been coding him?" Dr. Dutton asked.

"Twenty minutes," Dr. McGee said.

"Give another amp of bicarb," Dr. Dutton said.

CPR continued for another thirty minutes with Dr. Dutton taking over chest compressions without any change in the patient.

"I'm calling it," Dr. Dutton said, as she stopped chest compressions and looked around the room. "If we somehow brought him back he'd be a vegetable."

"I'll call his family, and see if they want an autopsy," Dr. McGee said, as she walked to the door.

"I don't think he has any family, but there may be a contact number on his chart," Susan said, "I had him last week, and I never saw anyone come to visit him."

"I'll see what I can find out," Dr. McGee said and she walked out of the room.

"How did he pull out his tube?" Dr. Dutton asked, as she looked at his arms, which were still tied to the bed.

"I have no idea," Henry said with exasperation, as he pulled on one of the restraints. "I had them tied as tight as I could without hurting him to make sure he couldn't extubate himself."

"Leave everything as it is," Dr. Dutton said and then added, "With all the mysterious things that have been happening on 3N, I'm going to call Ted Maxwell and have him come in to investigate this death."

"Do you think someone deliberately pulled his tube out?" Henry asked.

"I don't know," she said, "I'm not an investigator, but I want to find out if someone did this or not."

"I'll pull the curtain and slide the door closed," Henry said.

"Call me when Ted arrives," Dr. Dutton said and she walked off the floor.

Henry pulled the curtain around the bed, turned the lights off, and slid the glass door closed. Then he went back to the nurses' station to document what had just occurred.

Chapter 19

I arrived at the hospital at a quarter after one in the morning and went straight to the MICU nurse's desk. I stood at the counter looking at the nurses as they worked for several seconds without anyone noticing me being there. Then I cleared my throat and asked, "Can I speak to the nurse who had the patient that died earlier tonight?"

A man in his early forties stood up and said, "I had the patient," and then he asked, "Can I help you?"

"I'm Ted Maxwell with patient safety," I said. "I was called by Dr. Dutton and asked to investigate the death."

"My name is Henry Alexander," the man said, as he went to the phone and picked it up. "Dr. Dutton wanted me to call her when you got here," and he punched in a phone number.

I watched as Henry talked in a low voice on the phone for a few minutes then he put it down and said, "She'll be here in a moment."

"Thanks," I said, as I looked around the nurses' station and asked, "Do you have coffee made anywhere?"

"Sure, it's in the first room to your right," Henry said, as he started walking in that direction. "I made it about an hour ago," as he unlocked and opened the door.

"Great, it should still be good," I said, as I picked up a cup and poured some coffee in it.

"Do you want cream or sugar?"

"No, I drink it black, but thanks anyway."

"What did Dr. Dutton tell you?" Henry asked.

"She just said the patient died under mysterious conditions," I said, as I stopped at the door and asked, "Were you the one who found the patient?"

"Susan and I went to the room at the same time," he said.

"Why would both of you be checking on the patient together?"

"The monitor kept alarming. She didn't think that I was reacting quickly enough, so she got up to check on him herself," he said and rolled his eyes. "I told her he was my patient and I would check on him. So, we got to the room at the same time."

"What did you find when you got there?"

"His ET tube was lying on the floor, and he was unresponsive."

"Did he pull it out?"

"I don't see how he could," he said, "His hands were tied against the bedrails."

"Is that why she called me?"

"I think so."

I turned when I heard a knock at the door. Dr. Dutton was standing, looking through the glass, waiting for someone to open the door.

I opened it and asked, "Do you want some coffee?"

"Not now," she said, "I'm going to try to get some sleep after I talk to you."

"Do you want to go to the patient's room?" I asked.

"Sure," she said, turning to walk down the hall. I followed her to the room.

When we got there, she slid the door open and we walked inside. Dr. Dutton turned the lights on and we walked around the curtain.

She walked up to the bed and pointed at the patient's arms and said, "As you can see, he couldn't have moved his arms up to his mouth."

I took the restraint that was on his left arm and pulled to see how far it would stretch. Then I went to his right arm and did the same thing. Neither restraint moved more than an inch.

I shook my head and said, "No, he couldn't have reached the tube with his hands."

"I called you because of the mysterious deaths on 3N," Dr. Dutton said, "I don't want things to get out of hand."

"What have you heard about 3N?"

"I heard two patients died under mysterious circumstances."

"Did you hear any details?"

"No. Just that two people died and there are rumors that they may have been murdered."

I put on a pair of gloves and moved up to the head of the bed. I looked at the strip of tape that was dangling from the side of his face. Then I picked up the tube off the floor and examined the tape attached to it.

Both edges were smooth and appeared to be cleanly cut, so I measured them together to see if they would match. As I put the tape together, I looked to Dr. Dutton and said, "Look at the clean edges on this tape. It looks like it was cut."

"That's why I called you," said Dr. Dutton, "I just got a

bad feeling about this."

"I do too," I said. "I think I need to get the police involved this time."

"It's going to be hard to keep this quiet with the police at the hospital."

"I know, but I don't have a choice," I said, "I need someone here that can gather evidence and catch whoever did this."

"Three unexplained deaths in a week- the press is going to have a field day," she said as she walked toward the door.

I straightened the curtain back around the bed, then walked to the door and opened it. She turned the light off as we walked out of the room and I closed the door behind us.

"I need to call the police," I said as I took my cell phone out of my pocket.

"I'll leave this up to you," she said, "I'm going to get some sleep," and she walked away.

I called Mark and told him we had another suspicious death in the hospital. I asked him to be as discreet as possible when he got here so the rest of the patient's wouldn't be frightened. He said to give him thirty minutes and assured me that he would be as quiet as possible and hung up the phone.

After I put my cell phone away, I went to the break room and used the code that Henry had given me to get inside. I poured a cup of coffee and sat down at the table to gather my thoughts.

A few minutes later Henry walked in the break room and asked, "When do you want us to wrap the body?"

"Has the family been by?" I asked.

"He didn't have family," he said, "He was one of our homeless patients."

"I have someone coming by to talk to about the case

before you wrap the body."

"Admitting wants to know when we can clear the room for another patient," he said.

"Tell them it will be a couple more hours."

"They won't be happy."

"That's not my problem," I said and took a sip of coffee.

"Alright," he said, as he rushed out the door.

I poured another cup of coffee and walked to the nurses' desk.

Henry was on the phone trying to explain why the room wasn't available for a patient that was in the emergency room. He listened intently to the person on the other line and then he said, "I have no choice. The room has a dead body in it, and I can't just roll it out in the hall."

He listened some more and then he said, "I'll do the best I can," and he hung the phone up.

"They giving you a hard time?" I asked.

"Yes, they said they had a live body in the emergency room that needed the room more than the dead body did."

"The police are coming by to investigate Mr. Sims' death, so don't let anyone in that room until they get here," I said with a stern look on my face.

"Are you not going to be here?" he asked.

"Yes, I will but I need to go to my office for a few minutes," I said and added, "Call me as soon as they get here," as I walked away.

Chapter 20

When I got back to the floor, I saw John Swain with hospital security standing beside Detective Mark Stone as they leaned against the counter in deep discussion. They turned when they noticed me approaching.

Mark smiled and stepped toward me as he stuck his hand out while asking, "How have you been doing Ted?"

I shook his hand and answered, "I'd be doing better if they'd quit calling me at home to tell me that bad things are happening in the hospital."

"There does seem to be a lot of bad things happening," Mark agreed.

"That's true, and it's not making my job very easy," I said then I turned to John and said, "Thanks for bringing Mark to the floor."

"No problem," he said, "It gave me something to do besides watching the door for potential danger."

"I hope you didn't leave the door unattended."

"No, Gracie is at the door," he said, "But I guess I do need to get back down there," and he walked away.

After he was gone, Mark looked at me and asked, "Do you really think this guy was murdered?"

"Yes, I do."

"Why?"

"Because somebody cut the tape that was holding the endotracheal tube in place and laid it beside him."

"Are you sure it was cut?"

"Look for yourself when we get in the room."

"Is this the person we are waiting for?" Mark asked, as he looked down the hall.

I looked in the direction Mark had turned and said, "That's him," and I smiled.

Dr. Garland Bennett forced a smile as he approached but didn't say anything until he could talk without everyone else hearing. Then he asked in a low voice, "Is this another overdose?"

"No, this time a patient's endotracheal tube was removed and he suffocated," I whispered.

Mark moved a little closer and said, "Look, you ask me to come by and look at a potential murder scene. I didn't bring anyone here to gather evidence."

"I wanted both of you to see the patient before I reported it as a murder," I said, as I started toward the room. "If we all agree that it was murder, then I'll want you to call whomever you have to in order to launch a full investigation."

There was a cart placed outside the room with gowns and gloves for everyone to put on before they entered the room. We stopped and got appropriately dressed. Then we walked inside the room, turned the lights on, and closed the door behind us.

Dr. Bennett was the first to approach the patient. He carefully leaned over the side rail of the bed as he examined the tape that remained on the patient's face. Then he picked the endotracheal tube up and matched the ends of tape together and said, "They fit perfectly together."

Mark was standing on the other side of the bed watching everything that Dr. Bennett had done. He shook his head and said, "The tape was cut with something."

Dr. Bennett took the patient's arm and tried to pull it away from the side rail.

He could only move it about an inch before it was stopped with the restraint. Then he laid the arm down and said, "There's no way the patient cut the tape."

Mark looked at Dr. Bennett, then looked at me and announced, "Gentlemen this is a murder case. I need to call our CSI unit to look for evidence," and he walked out of the room.

Dr. Bennett stepped to the foot of the bed and said, "He has rigor mortis setting in," and he pointed to the patient's left arm and added, "The restraint stopped me from moving his arm toward his face, but I had to put a lot of force into moving it as little as I did."

"What should we do?"

"Just leave the body here until the CSI unit gathers evidence," he said, "I'll fix everything when I get him in the morgue," and he stepped out of the room.

I follow and closed the door.

As we were taking our gown and gloves off, Mark closed his phone and said, "The CSI unit should be here in thirty minutes."

I looked at the nurses' desk where several people were standing in a circle, glancing in our direction from time to time as they talked.

"Let's go in their break room and have a cup of coffee

while we wait," I said and I walked toward the break room.

I used the code that Henry have given me and opened the door. Mark and Dr. Bennett walked in first and sat at a small round table that was in the center of the room. I went to the coffee pot and started a fresh pot of coffee. Then I sat down at the table to wait for it to brew.

"How are Sara and the kids doing?" Mark asked, trying to make conversation.

"They're fine," I answered. "They went to Sara's mothers for a couple of weeks."

"I hope nothing is wrong."

"No, they're fine," I said, "They go to her house for two weeks every year," and I got up and poured a cup of coffee before continuing, "I usually try to join them for a couple of days, but with these murders, I told Sara that I wouldn't be able to join them this year."

"It's probably better that the kids are not nearby to hear about the murders."

"I guess so, but they'll be back in a couple of days," I said then asked, "What about you Mark? Are you seeing anyone, or are you still determined to be a bachelor?"

"Ted, you know I'm married to my job," he answered with a laugh. Then his face got serious as he added, "I wouldn't expect anyone to put up with the kind of hours I have to work and the uncertainty that this job requires."

"What happened to you and Jan Mosley?"

"She got tired of the long nights alone," he said as he stared off in the distance.

I dropped the subject as I poured coffee for everyone and sat down to wait for the CSI crew to arrive.

Chapter 21

After the second cup of coffee, I got up and said, "It's about time for them to get here, so let's go to the nurses' desk and wait," and I walked to the door. I stood with my hand on the door knob and watched as Mark got up and walked toward the trash can.

He finished his coffee and threw the cup away. Then he walked to the door and stopped.

I opened the door and held it as Mark walked out into the hall.

Dr. Bennett poured what was left in his cup in the sink and threw the empty cup in the trash. Then he followed Mark out into the hall.

I followed Dr. Bennett and closed the door behind me.

"I hope they get here soon," Dr. Bennett said, "I have a lot of work to do today, and I'd like to start on the autopsy as soon as I can," and he started walking toward the nurses desk.

"It shouldn't be long," I said and I leaned up against the counter when we got to the nurses' desk.

Mark stood beside me with his back against the counter as

he looked down the hall in the direction the CSI unit would arrive.

Dr. Bennett eased over to where the heart monitor was located and stood watching a nurse as she sat in front of it staring at the patient's heart rhythm. He watched her for a few seconds before she sensed his presence and looked up.

He smiled and asked, "Can I have a copy of the lab results that were drawn on the deceased patient?"

"What?" she asked, as she looked around the nurses' desk to see who was listening.

"I need a copy of the lab results that were drawn during the code."

Her eyes widened as she tried to decide whether to give the results or not.

Dr. Bennett took his name tag and turned it around so she could see his name and the hospital logo. "I'm Dr. Bennett with the department of pathology," he said and smiled. "I'll need the results when I perform the autopsy later on today."

"Don't you have access to a computer in the pathologist lab?" she asked.

"Yes I do," he said, "But it would save me some time if I had them already available when I got to the lab."

"Alright, which labs do you want?"

"I need lab results from the past forty-eight hours."

"Alright, give me a minute," she said and she rolled her chair to a computer. She clicked a couple of buttons and the printer erupted into life and started shooting sheets of paper into the holding tray.

When the printer stopped, she got up and took the sheets of paper out of the holding tray. Then she handed them to Dr. Bennett and asked, "Are these all the labs you needed?"

He took the papers and scanned through each one. Then

he shook his head yes and said, "This is exactly what I asked for. Thank you so much."

"Anytime," she said, as she smiled and went back to her chair in front of the monitor.

Dr. Bennett slid the lab results in the side pocket of his folder and tucked it under his left arm.

Mark took a step away from the counter and said, "Here they are."

I looked down the hall where two men wearing dark green scrubs were effortlessly walking toward us carrying a large tackle box in each hand. Following them was a man wearing faded blue jeans carrying a large container in his right hand.

Mark pointed toward them and said, "The two wearing green scrubs are from the CSI unit. The one on the left is Roger Farris and the one on the right is Justin Wells. The man in jeans is Glen Watts, our forensic pathologist."

"Why is he here?" I asked.

"I'm not sure," Mark said, "I didn't call him."

"Where is the victim?" Roger asked in a low voice, as he leaned close to Mark.

"I'll show you," Mark said and he started walking toward the victim's room.

Glen Watts stuck his hand out and said, "I'm Glen Watts."

I shook his hand and said, "I'm Ted Maxwell with patient safety in the hospital."

He looked at Dr. Bennett and said, "Dr. Bennett, it's good to see you again."

"Glen it looks like you've done well for yourself," he said.

Glen smiled and said, "I've done alright," and he took a step closer and added, "I hope you don't mind, but I was with these guys when they were called and I thought I might like to sit in on the autopsy."

"Sure, I can use all the help I can get," Dr. Bennett said.

"I want to look at the body," Glen said, as he went toward the victim's room.

I turned to Dr. Bennett and said, "It sounded like you two knew each other."

"He was my student many years ago."

"Why did he leave?"

"Budget cuts took his position away and he went to work for the county while he continued his education."

"Was he bitter?"

"No I don't think so, because we both believe that everything happens for a reason," he said, "He actually had more time for school when he changed jobs."

"Let's see what they are doing," I said, as I started walking down the hall.

Mark and Glen were standing outside the room watching the CSI guys as they were dusting for fingerprints.

"That's not going to do any good," I said. "I bet there are over fifty different sets of fingerprints in that room."

"That may be true, but one of them may belong to the killer," Mark said.

"If people wore gloves like they are supposed to, there wouldn't be that many sets," Dr. Bennett said.

"Actually, the hospital has been trying to persuade everyone to stop using gloves unless they are handling bodily fluids," I said, "It helps cut the cost of supplies and also maintains a more personal touch."

"I don't think that sounds very sanitary."

"Our new policy encourages everyone to wash their hands after every encounter and to really scrub if they come in contact with bodily fluids."

"Gloves must really be expensive."

"We have the potential to save over a million dollars this year," I said, as I stepped close to the door to watch the CSI crew gather evidence.

I watched Roger Farris as he cut the tubing away from the ventilator and placed it in a glass container.

Justin Wells bent down and meticulously looked at something on the floor using a magnifying glass. Then he got a pair of tweezers out of his tackle box and carefully picked the object up. After bringing it close to his eyes and studying it for a few seconds, he placed it in a glass vial, screwing the black top tight and placed it in his tackle box.

As the CSI crew prepared to go, they took one last look around the room before gathering their tackle boxes and walking into the hall.

"Did you find anything?" I asked with excitement.

Roger looked at Mark without saying anything.

"It's alright, you can tell him what you found," Mark said. "We're going to be working this case together."

"Alright," Roger said, "We found twenty-five sets of fingerprints throughout the room, a small blood smear along the side rail of the bed and a small dirt sample at the base of the ventilator. Oh, and I took the tubing off the ventilator that was still attached to the endotracheal tube."

"What about the tape that is on the victim?" I asked.

"Oh, I'll get that off when I do the autopsy and have Glen take it to the CSI lab," Dr. Bennett interjected.

"Well guys, we still have a lot of work to do here," Roger said. "We need to fingerprint all the nurses that went into the victim's room as well as the doctors," and he started walking toward the nurse's desk.

Justin followed.

I went with them and explained the situation to the nurses

at the desk. After they all agreed to be fingerprinted, I called the doctor's call room and told Dr. Dutton that everyone that entered the room must come to the nurses' desk to be fingerprinted.

Dr. Bennett had called the morgue attendant while I was on the phone with Dr. Dutton and asked him to come with a gurney to take the body away.

The morgue attendant was the first to arrive on the floor. He went straight to the room and began loading the body.

Dr. Dutton and Dr. McGee came shortly after and stopped at the front of the nurse's desk.

They watched as the morgue attendant rolled the body past the nurses' desk toward the end of the hall. Then Dr. Dutton asked, "Where do we need to go?"

"They're setup in the break room," Henry said, as he walked toward the doctors and pointed down the hall.

"Thanks," Dr. Dutton said and they walked toward the break room.

"I've got work to do," Dr. Bennett said and he walked away.

Glen Watts followed as he went toward the elevators.

I looked around the nurses' desk where everyone was busy performing their early morning duties. They were printing lab slips and gathering tubes in preparation for drawing blood. Some were pulling medications from the med room and mixing them together with fluids to be infused through the patient's central line.

"Hey, Henry," I said, as he walked past.

"What can I help you with?" he asked.

"I need a list of everyone that worked yesterday," I said. "They will need to be fingerprinted."

"Give me a minute, and I'll print the schedule," he said

and he walked to a computer.

Dr. Dutton and Dr. McGee came out of the break room and walked off the floor. Then Roger and Justin stepped out into the hall with a tackle box in each hand and quickly approached the desk.

Henry handed me a sheet of paper and said, "This is everyone that worked yesterday."

I took the paper and glanced at the names. "Do you know when they work again?" I asked.

"Everyone should work today," he said, "We work three days in a row and yesterday started the week."

I handed the list to Roger and said, "These people will need to be fingerprinted today."

He took the list, folded it, and stuck it in his pocket.

"Let's go get some breakfast," Mark said, "Then we'll come back and catch them before they get too busy."

"Sounds good," Roger said.

"I'd like to put some of this equipment in the van and not have to carry it everywhere we go," Justin said.

"When we come back, we'll just bring what we need to fingerprint everyone," Roger said, as he started walking toward the elevator.

"Ted, do you want to come with us?" Mark asked.

I looked at the clock which indicated that it was five thirty in the morning and said, "I could use something good to eat," and we walked to the elevator. We went to the first floor, walked out the sliding glass doors at the front of the hospital and drove to a small restaurant that specializes in breakfast.

Chapter 22

Hanna Johns, Westbrook Medical Center's chief nursing officer, and Elizabeth Pitch, nurse manager for the Medical Intensive Care Unit, were standing at the nurses' station waiting for us to arrive. They turned toward us as we approached but said nothing until we were close enough to hear without them speaking very loud.

"Why did you bring the police here?" Hanna Johns demanded between clinched teeth.

"I needed help with a murder," I calmly responded.

"Who said the patient was murdered?"

"I did."

"I guess you're an expert on these kinds of things since the incidences on 3N."

"I asked Detective Mark Stone to look at the patient and help me determine if it was murder."

"And what did he determine?"

"The patient sure didn't cut the tape and pull the endotracheal tube out of his mouth himself," Mark said, as he stepped forward.

I looked at Elizabeth Pitch as her head began to bobble

from early stages of Parkinson's disease and she took a step forward and resentfully proclaimed, "You're out of your mind if you think my nurses are going to let you take their fingerprints."

"Elizabeth, we asked everyone to let us get a sample of their fingerprints to help rule them out as being a suspect," I explained. "If they don't want to let us, then Mark can take them to jail for obstructing justice."

"He wouldn't dare."

Mark smiled without saying anything.

"It would be easier to cooperate," I said, as I looked at Roger and Justin and added, "Go set up in the break room."

They walked down the hall and went into the break room.

"You're just trying to show your authority," Elizabeth said, as she moved a little closer to my face. "And you have no authority on this floor."

"You might want to check my job description," I said, as I smiled. "It states that I have full authority over the entire hospital as long as it pertains to the well-being of our patients."

"This is my floor!" she demanded.

"Just fingerprint the nurses," Hanna said, "But do it as quickly and quietly as possible."

"Start sending them in the break room two at a time and everything will be done within a matter of minutes," I said, as I looked across the nurses' desk at several nurses that were watching from a distance.

Elizabeth turned to Hanna and said, "I don't like this."

"I don't either," Hanna said, "But there's not much we can do about it."

"Patient care is being interrupted for no good reason."

"It might help us find the killer," I said.

Elizabeth glared at me for a few seconds before turning to a nurse that was standing by the printer and saying, "Send two people into the break room to be fingerprinted."

The nurse jumped to attention and hurried to a group of nurses that were sitting in the back.

After a few seconds, two of the nurses walked around the nurses' desk and went into the break room.

I watched as everyone filed into the break room two at a time until everyone was fingerprinted.

After the last two nurses exited the break room, Roger and Justin slowly walked to the nurses' desk carrying their tackle boxes.

Elizabeth demanded, "Are you finished disrupting my floor?"

"At the moment, but we'll be back if we have any questions," I said and we started walking toward the elevator.

Hanna rushed toward us and asked in a low voice, "You are going to keep this quiet aren't you?"

"I'm trying to keep this as quiet as possible," I said, "But this time I needed some help."

"Alright, just do the best you can to keep it out of the media," she said nervously.

"I will," I said.

"This hospital doesn't need any bad publicity," she said, as she walked away.

When she was several feet away, Mark whispered, "That nurse manager really doesn't like you."

"Who doesn't like me? Elizabeth Pitch?" I asked.

"I guess. It's the nurse manager on this floor."

"Yeah, we didn't get along before I got the job of patient safety officer, but after I got the job she's really been hostile toward me."

"Why does she not like you?"

"I think she got angry because Larry Adcock hand-picked me for the job and didn't give her a chance to apply," I answered.

"That was Larry Adcock's decision, not yours," Mark said. "If she's mad at anyone it should be him."

"Another possible reason is that I discovered that several of her nurses weren't following hospital protocol and brought it to her attention. Now she gets angry every time she sees me," I said, "I think she feels intimidated by me and that makes her angry."

"She should have been happy that you told her."

"She wanted to think that her nurses were perfect, and by me pointing out a discrepancy she took that as a slur against her," I said, "She thought I was criticizing her management skills," and I looked down the hall.

I watched Hanna Johns as she went to the nurses' desk and disappeared around the corner. Then we went to the elevator and rode down to the second floor to wait in my office for Dr. Bennett to inform us of the results from the autopsy.

Chapter 23

Dr. Bennett and Glen Watts arrived at my office about thirty minutes after we got there. They stopped at the door and looked around the room for a place to sit.

"Wait a minute, and I'll get you a chair," I said as I went into the lobby and dragged a chair through the door.

Dr. Bennett took that chair and sat it in front of my desk.

I got another chair and placed it against the wall close to the door.

"Thanks," Glen said, as he sat down and placed a plastic box on the floor beside him.

Everyone turned their attention to Dr. Bennett as they waited for him to begin his report on the autopsy. He shuffled a few sheets of paper, and then he said, "The patient died as we thought he did. He died because someone removed his endotracheal tube which removed his ability to breathe."

"Did you see any signs of a struggle?" Mark asked.

"He didn't have the ability to struggle because he was tied to the bed," Dr. Bennett said then he added, "Part of his lungs were filled with fluid, but the majority of his lungs were consolidated from pneumonia. He apparently had a long history of pneumonia and his lungs developed scar tissue which prevented air from moving back and forth through his lungs."

"Did you find anything else?" I asked.

"Yes, he had track marks on his arms which indicated that he was an IV drug abuser."

"Did that contribute to his pneumonia?"

"Possibly, but the majority of his pneumonia was caused because he lived on the street," he said, "He was exposed to a multitude of diseases from other homeless people as well as exposing them to whatever he had been carrying."

"Did you find any evidence that would help us catch the killer?"

"I got the tape off the victim's face so it could be matched with what was on the tube, but I really didn't find anything to help catch the killer."

"Glen, do you have anything to add?" I asked.

"No, I agree with everything that Dr. Bennett had to say," he said, as he picked up the plastic box and added, "I have the tape from the victim's face in here."

Roger stood up and said, "We need to get back to the CSI lab to start analyzing what evidence we have," and he walked toward the door.

Justin got up and followed.

I got up and opened the door. "Thanks for all your help," I said.

"No problem," Roger said and he walked out.

"We're glad to help," Justin said, as he followed Roger out the door.

"Thanks for letting me watch the autopsy," Glen said, as he shook Dr. Bennett's hand. "I always enjoy seeing a pro at work," he added, as he walked out the door.

I looked at Dr. Bennett who was smiling when Glen left.

He stopped smiling when he realized I was watching him and said, "I need to get back to work," and he stood up.

"What was that look you gave Glen when he left?" I asked.

"It was a proud look," he said, "He has really developed into a very good forensic pathologist, and I believe I played a large part in his development. Now if you're finished badgering me, I need to get to work," and he walked out the door.

Mark stood up and said, "I need to go, too. Call me if you find any information," and he left.

I closed the door and sat down at my desk. Then I booted the computer up and started working on my report of the morning's events.

Chapter 24

Tony Boswell sat down beside Hanna Johns as she ate her breakfast in the hospital cafeteria. He leaned in close and whispered, "I heard you had some excitement this morning."

She glanced around frantically to see who was close by and might be listening. Then she asked, "Where did you hear that?"

"Faye, my secretary, told me the police were here when I walked into my office this morning."

"How did she know?"

"Apparently Gus Mills, head of hospital security, called Larry Adcock this morning to get permission to let the police onto the floor to investigate the murder and he was complaining about it to his secretary," Tony said and smiled. "And of course she told Faye as soon as she got to the office."

"I hope this doesn't get all over the hospital," Hanna said, as she suddenly lost her appetite and pushed her plate to the center of the table.

"I think it's mainly in the administration offices right now."

"What are they saying?"

"Faye said that some of the secretaries believe the patient was killed because he didn't have insurance."

"That's ridiculous," she said, "We don't target patients on their ability to pay."

"Do you remember what Larry said at our last business meeting?"

"Yes, I remember, but he didn't mean to have them killed."

"Are you sure?" he asked with a smirk on his face.

"Well," she said, as she looked Tony in the eyes and added, "I don't think that's what he meant."

"I don't think he meant for us to kill the patients either, but there were a lot of people at our meeting and they may have interpreted it differently."

"All I can think of is how the hospital is going to handle this," she said, "I know I should feel bad about the patient, but I don't."

"He was a leech, bleeding the hospital of its revenue," Tony said. "It's hard to feel bad when someone like him dies."

"I still must put up a front and pretend to be really remorseful because the hospital has a reputation to protect," she said, as she took a sip of coffee.

"That's one of your best qualities," he said, "You can act like you care when you really don't."

"I've had a lot of practice in my career," she said, as she stood up and added, "Now the show begins," and she carried her tray to the trash can.

Tony got up and followed her as she threw her trash away. "I'll see you later," he said.

"I'll see you at lunch," she said, "I need to make rounds

on the floors and pretend to care about my nurses," and she laughed.

"They will work harder if they think you care about them," Tony said.

"Yes, they will," she said and smiled, then added, "And that can help delay our need for giving raises," and she walked away.

Chapter 25

As I filled out the report on the murder of Rick Sims, I continued to wonder why anyone would kill a defenseless man. Then I remembered the victims on 3N and questioned if they were connected. Were they killed by the same person, or should I be looking for more than one killer? I shuddered as I thought of the possibility of having three killers on the loose in the hospital.

I finished putting in the last details in my report and clicked the save button when my phone started ringing. I picked it up as a message flashed across my computer screen acknowledging that my file had been saved and said, "Ted speaking. How can I help you?"

"Hey, Ted, this is Garland Bennett," a male voice said, "I think you need to go to the basement."

"What's going on?"

"I just got a call from security reporting a dead body hanging from the conveyor system."

"OH MY GOD!" I exclaimed. "Is it a patient?"

"No, I don't think so," he said, "I think it's someone that works here, but I haven't been down there yet to see."

"I'll meet you in the basement," I said, as I put the phone down on the receiver and rushed out of my office.

I bypassed the elevators and went straight to the stairs. Trying to get there as fast as I could, I took two steps at a time as I went down the stairs.

As I pushed the door open and walked into the basement, I immediately looked in the direction of the conveyor system for the body. The body was nowhere in sight, so I slowly started walking down the long hall toward the supply storeroom.

I heard the voices of two men talking as I was about to turn the corner of the hall and I stopped. I listened for several seconds to see if I could recognize their voices.

One man had a high pitched voice and the other had a deep, rumbly voice. The high pitched voice I recognized as that of John Swain with hospital security, so I stepped around the corner of the hall and asked, "Where's the body?"

John stopped talking and pointed directly in front of him toward the conveyor system without saying anything.

I looked in the direction he was pointing and saw a limp body hanging upside down from a hook that was attached to the conveyor system. A chain was wrapped around the victim's right leg and it was hoisted up to the ceiling like a cow ready for slaughter.

As I neared the body, I saw a large circle of blood directly below the victim. Dangling from the ceiling, the body appeared to be a man, but I couldn't see his face. So, I leaned in close to see if I recognized who it was. He was wearing a uniform, which indicated that he worked for the hospital, but his shirt dropped down and covered his face to conceal his identity. As I looked at his small frame, I realized that his body type could have been that of several employees of the hospital.

Since I couldn't get a good view of the victim without touching anything, I backed against the wall and stood beside John to wait for Garland Bennett to arrive.

"Could you tell who it is?" John asked.

"No. I couldn't see his face," I said and turned when Garland stepped around the corner.

He stood looking at the victim for a few seconds, then he slipped on a pair of gloves and slowly walked toward the body.

As he neared the body, he carefully stepped around the pool of blood and grabbed the victim's shirt. He slowly lifted it over the victim's head to reveal his face and asked, "Do you know this guy?" and he looked back at me.

I stepped forward and looked at the victim. "Yes, that's Leo Brown. He works in the supply warehouse," I said, as I stepped back to the wall and added, "He delivered the fluid to 3N that had heparin mixed in the bags."

"It looks like somebody wanted to keep him quiet," Garland said, as he pointed to the victim's neck. "They slit his throat."

I looked at Garland when I heard the motor that controls the conveyor belt turn on and the chain began to tighten.

He glared at John and demanded, "Turn the motor off!"

"I thought it was off," John said, as he ran to the control panel and flipped the main switch off.

Everything stopped at once. The lights went off which left us in total darkness. I could hear everyone breathing as they inhaled at once from the shock of the situation.

A bright light emerged from the control panel as John took his flashlight off his belt and turned it on. "I'll get the lights on in a minute," he said, as he shined his flashlight toward the panel and looked for the right switch to turn on.

He flipped two switches then he turned the main power back on which brought instant light back to the basement. I looked at Garland with an arched brow as the motors remained quiet.

"I had to stop it the fastest way I knew how," John said, as he walked back toward us with a sheepish look on his face.

"I hate to say it, but we need to get the police down here to see if they can find any evidence," Garland said.

"I'll call Mark Stone, and tell him of our situation," I said, as I took my cell phone out of my pocket and stepped away from everyone.

Within minutes, I had arranged for Mark and the CSI unit to discreetly come to the hospital.

I put my phone back in my pocket and walked back to the group of men that were standing against the wall looking at the victim as he hung from the ceiling.

"Do you have the police coming?" Garland asked.

"Yes, they should be here in about thirty minutes," I said.

"Good, I'll get a stretcher so we'll be ready to take the body down when they are finished," Garland said and he walked away.

After Garland was out of sight, I stepped close to John and asked, "Who found the body?"

John looked at the man that was standing beside him and said, "He did."

"What is your name?" I asked, as I looked at his face.

"Roy Green," he said.

"Why were you in the basement?"

"Someone called my office and reported a problem with the system," he said, as he pointed at the conveyor belt. "I have a contract with the hospital to keep it running."

"Did you find a problem when you got here?"

"The system runs fine," he said, "The only problem I found was the dead boy hanging from the ceiling."

"What did you do when you saw the body?"

"I called John."

"And John, what did you do when he called you?"

"I came down to see what he was talking about then I called you," John said.

"Did either of you touch anything?"

"I might have stepped in the blood," Roy said, "But I didn't touch anything with my hands."

"I stayed away from the body," John said and shivered then added, "I hate dead bodies."

"They don't bother me as long as you keep their head covered like his head is covered, but if I see a face I think I'm being watched," Roy said, as he leaned against the wall and looked away from the victim.

I looked at my watch and said, "They should be here any minute," and I walked around the corner to see if they were getting off the elevator.

John followed me and asked, "Do I need to stay here?"

"Mark might want to talk to you before you leave," I said.

"Alright I'll stay," he said, as he walked back to where Roy was standing and leaned against the wall beside him.

I followed and stood beside them to wait for the police to arrive.

"Is that them," John asked, as we heard a loud banging noise come from the direction of the elevators.

"I think it's Garland bringing the stretcher," I said, as I heard the clanging noise of the wheels as it bounced along the hard surface of the basement.

Within seconds, Garland rounded the corner with the

stretcher and pushed it against the wall beside where we were standing.

I looked behind Garland and saw Mark Stone and the same two CSI men that were with him when Rick Sims was murdered.

They looked at me for a second then turned their heads toward the victim hanging from the ceiling.

Justin Wells put on a pair of gloves, then approached the body and said, "This hospital is a dangerous place to be."

"How do you want to do this?" Roger Farris asked, as he slipped on a pair of gloves.

"I know we can't take this entire system to the lab, but let's at least take the chain that's wrapped around the victim's leg and dust the area for prints," Justin said, "We may also want to look for whatever tool the killer used to put the victim up on that hook."

"He had to stand on something to be able to reach that high," Roger said, as he looked along the floor for whatever device the killer used.

"First, I think I'll get a sample of this blood to make sure it is the victim's," Justin said, as he took a cotton swab and scooped up a sample of blood. He then put it in a glass vial and screwed the lid tight.

"Who found the body?" Mark asked, as he turned away from the victim and brought his attention to me.

"His name is Roy Green," I said, as I pointed to him.

Mr. Green stepped forward and said, "I found the body hanging from the conveyor system."

"Why were you at the hospital?" Mark asked.

"Like I said before, I was called and told the system was down," he said. "I have a contract with the hospital to keep this system running at all times."

"Did you see anyone strange when you got to the basement?"

"I saw a lot of strange people, but I think they all work for the hospital," he said and smiled then he lowered his head and added, "I'm sorry. I shouldn't have made that comment."

Mark looked at me and mumbled, "He's right about strange people working at the hospital," and he turned his eyes toward John who was intently watching the CSI crew as they gathered evidence.

"Back to what you asked," Mr. Green said, "I didn't see anyone that didn't look like they worked here."

"Mr. Green, I guess you can go," Mark said, as he gave him his card and added, "Call me if you think of anything else."

"Thanks," he said, as he took the card and walked away.

"This is what he used to hoist the body up," Justin said, as he pointed to a wench that was bolted to the steel rail beside the conveyor system. "He placed the cable over the steel rail running along the ceiling and pulled the body up with the wench until it could be attached to the hook that's hanging down," and he started dusting it for prints.

"Maybe we can use that to lower the body onto the stretcher when you're through," Garland said.

"Hey, I think I see a trace of blood on the wiring," Justin said, as he took a cotton swab, wiped it along the wire and placed it in a glass vial, closing the lid tightly afterward.

"We probably need to carry that with us to the lab," Roger said, as he moved to where Justin was working.

"I think you're right," Justin said, as he stood up and added, "We can help you lower the body to the stretcher but I don't think we need this wench because its evidence."

Roger took a socket set out of his evidence box and

carefully started unbolting the wench from the steel rail. Then he slipped it in a large plastic bag and laid it on top of his evidence box. He turned to Mark and said, "It's too big to fit in my evidence box, so I guess you'll have to carry it for us."

"I'm here to help," Mark said.

"I think we've gotten everything we need," Justin said, "So, I guess we need to get the body down," and he pulled a wooden container over toward the body.

He turned it over and climbed on top to see if he could reach high enough to help get the chain off the hook and release the body from the ceiling.

Garland put on a pair of gloves and rolled the stretcher under the body. He locked the wheels and said, "The stretcher is ready if you can help get him off the hook."

I put on a pair of gloves and moved toward the body. I took the victim's shoulders to help guide the body onto the stretcher once he was dislodged from the hook.

Justin grabbed the victim's legs and tried to lift, but he couldn't lift the body high enough to release his leg.

So, Roger got on the wooden crate beside Justin and they both lifted the victim at the same time. This time they were able to lift the victim off the hook, and we carefully placed him on the stretcher.

Garland covered the victim with a sheet, and he rolled his body toward the elevators to be transported to the morgue.

"Here you go," Roger said, as he handed the wench to Mark.

"Thanks," Mark said, as he took it with both hands.

"Thank you for coming," I said.

"We'll let you know if we find anything," Justin said, as he picked up his evidence box and started toward the elevator.

Roger followed.

"If you keep calling me, I'm not going to be able to keep it quiet," Mark said, "This is developing into a very dangerous place to be."

"I know," I said.

"I'll call you if they find anything," Mark said, as he turned and walked to the elevators.

I watched them as they disappeared behind the elevator door, then I walked to the stairs, and slowly walked up to the second floor and went into my office.

Chapter 26

"I want to know what is going on in this hospital," Brian Dawson demanded, as he stormed into my office.

Brian Dawson came to Westbrook Medical Center five years ago, after he got his doctorate in hospital administration and was appointed director of surgery. He was hired to recruit the finest surgeons and maintain a reputation of excellence in all surgical fields to improve the clientele of the hospital and increase revenue.

With limited resources to offer the surgeons, his recruiting tactics were falling short, .and the surgeons with better reputations were taking positions in California and Washington. The fact that he couldn't entice qualified surgeons to come to Westbrook Medical Center and that his projected numbers were falling well short of the goal set by the hospital caused Brian Dawson to be short-tempered most of the time.

I minimized my computer screen without turning in his direction, then I slowly and calmly looked at him and asked, "What are you talking about?"

"You know what I'm talking about," he said, "Those

people on 3N were killed, then the person in the ICU, and now that poor kid killed himself in the basement."

I leaned back in my chair without saying anything for several seconds as I tried to determine what he was up to.

He leaned forward in his chair with his eyes glued to my face.

"That kid in the basement didn't commit suicide," I said, as I looked at his eyes. "But his death is still being investigated by the police, so I can't talk about it."

"You mean he didn't kill himself. I thought he was found hanging from the ceiling."

"Where did you get your information?"

"I asked John Swain, and he said a body was hanging from the ceiling."

"Well, as I said before, the police are still investigating, and I don't think they are considering suicide as a possible cause of death."

"Did you find anything that might help you catch the killer?"

"Why are you so interested?"

"I'm trying to look out for the well-being of the hospital and with all the deaths that have occurred, the hospital's going to get a bad reputation."

"I'm doing the best I can do," I said, as I sat up in my chair and leaned toward Mr. Dawson and added, "I don't need any help from you unless you can tell me the killer's name."

"I don't know who the killer is," he said.

"Then let me and the police do our jobs."

"I'm not trying to tell you how to do your job," he said angrily. "I just want you to handle this as quickly as possible so we can decrease the amount of damage the hospital has to suffer."

"I'm more concerned with the patients that are dying."

"Don't forget who pays your salary," he said as he stood up and walked to the door.

"I know who pays my salary, but I also know that my main responsibility is to the patients that I am paid to protect."

"Just keep it quiet while you're protecting the patients," he said and walked out.

I stared at the door for a few seconds in disbelief at what had just occurred. Then I turned back to my computer and got back to work.

Chapter 27

I finished my report and clicked the print button when I heard a knock at the door.

"What is it this time," I grumbled as I got up and opened the door.

"Are you busy?" Garland Bennett asked.

"I need to get the report off the printer and file it," I said, as I walked to the printer. "Then I'll have a few minutes."

I took a small stack of papers off the printer, looked at each one to make sure they were numbered consecutively and then put them in my filing cabinet. The clock on the wall indicated that he hadn't had time to do the autopsy, so I closed the drawer and asked, "Why are you here? I thought you'd still be doing the autopsy."

"Oh, the police thought the body should go to the forensic lab since the victim's death was obviously murder," he said and he looked at his watch then added, "Glen Watts was waiting in the morgue when I got there with the body."

"Are you okay with that?"

"I really didn't have a choice," he said, as he repositioned himself in the chair. "He had papers ordering me to release the body."

"Did he not trust your ability to do the job?"

"He said they had better facilities to run the tests and the results would hold up better in court."

"I can see that because a defense attorney would argue that you manipulated the evidence to help protect the hospital," I said, "This way it's unbiased."

"I wouldn't do that, but I know everyone wouldn't believe it because they don't know me."

"And the hospital does pay your salary," I said, as I closed the filing cabinet and sat down in my chair.

"That's true."

"Why did you come by?" I asked, as I leaned back in my chair. "Did you want anything?"

"I just wanted to tell you that you needed to be careful," he said, as he looked toward the door. "I think someone that works here is involved with these murders and not only with the patients, but also with the kid that was hanging from the conveyor system."

"Do you think I'm in danger?"

"I think it depends on how close you are to catching the killer."

"What do you mean?"

"If the killer feels in danger of getting caught then he might try to eliminate the threat."

"I see what you mean. I'll be careful." Then I asked, "Do you have any thoughts on who might be the killer?"

He glanced at the door again before saying, "I really don't have an idea. It could be almost anybody," then he moved closer and continued in a low voice, "I think the police gathered some evidence this morning that might help to catch the killer."

"I hope so," I said wishfully. "I feel like I'm getting a lot of pressure from the hospital directors to solve the murders quickly and to keep them quiet."

"Yes, I'm not so sure they care if we catch the killer," he said with a look of disgust on his face. "They just want it to be kept quiet so it doesn't affect future patient flow into the hospital and profits don't decline."

"It's all about money."

"Most everything is," he said, as he got up and walked to the door. "I'll talk to you later," and he walked out of my office.

I sat at my desk for a few minutes trying to absorb everything that Garland had warned me about, and I knew the potential danger that I might be putting myself in as the investigation proceeded. However, my job was to protect the patients, and I'd do everything in my power to do that. I just needed to be more observant of my surroundings when I walked around the hospital. After glancing at the clock one more time, I locked the filing cabinet, turned my computer off, and went home.

Chapter 28

Larry Adcock strolled into the hospital administration conference center wearing a light gray three piece suit, bright pink shirt with a baby blue tie tied with meticulous care around his neck. He sported a matching gray brief case, which he carried in his right hand.

As he made his way to the front of the room, he looked each hospital department director in the eyes and gave them a warm smile as he expressed his happiness that they were able to attend the meeting.

When he got to the front of the table, Tony Boswell leaned over to Hanna Johns and whispered, "I wonder what's got him in such a good mood?"

"I guess we'll find out in a minute," she responded and sat back as if she hadn't said anything.

When Mr. Adcock reached the head of the table, he placed his briefcase on top, opened it up, and took out a large stack of papers. He separated the stack into two sections and handed one to Kelly Adams, his trusted assistant who always sat on his right side and made sure everyone got handouts to help speed the meeting along.

Each director watched in awe at Kelly's efficiency and organization when they had a meeting. They didn't know how long she had worked for Larry Adcock, but they knew she had been with him long enough to know how to read his body language and be able to anticipate his needs. Each meeting was conducted as if it had been well-rehearsed.

The directors also knew that Kelly had access to more information in the administration offices than anyone else, so if they had a question they would go to her first. If she couldn't answer it, then they would turn to Larry Adcock. She was well respected and used as a great resource throughout the department.

Kelly stood up on cue, grabbed the stack of papers and began handing them out without a word being spoken. Then she took the other stack and proceeded to repeat the process.

Mr. Adcock moved to the podium as Kelly was passing out his notes and stood without saying a word until everyone had both sheets of paper in front of them and Kelly had sat back down.

Then he cleared his throat and announced, "I've handed out papers today because I thought this information needed to be in hard copy so everyone could retain it and use it to help find ways to improve our patient flow process."

He picked up the remote and clicked on the slide machine. As the screen brightened and a graph came into view, he picked up the pointer and said happily, "As you can see in the first column, our profits have started improving over the last week," and he pointed to a column colored in green.

Then he pointed to the second column and said, "As you can see here, we have had fewer uninsured patient days," and he looked around the room and added, "And I contribute this to our efficiency in discharging patients without insurance."

He clicked to another screen and said, "We're still in the red, but if things continue to improve we should be in the black by the end of our physical year," and he laid the pointer on the podium and walked to the head of the table and continued, "We still have room to improve, but we're headed in the right direction."

He pulled his chair out, sat down, and said, "At the end of our last meeting I asked everyone to have a plan ready to help us control the influx of uninsured patients in our hospital and suggestions as to how we can decrease their hospital stays," then he asked, "Does anyone have any suggestions on how we can continue to persuade our uninsured to go elsewhere?"

He looked at each director for a response.

Hanna Johns stood up and said, "I think we should keep doing what we are doing by discharging them as soon as possible and getting them an appointment with the free clinic for follow up."

Tony Boswell laughed and said, "I think the word has gotten out on the street that people are being killed if they don't have insurance and that has persuaded several people to go to other hospitals."

"I hope not our paying customers," Larry Adcock said indignantly. "It is our fundamental mission to have as many paying patients go through our hospital as possible to increase our profit."

"Our census has declined a lot over the past week," Kelly Adams interjected.

Larry Adcock's expression changed from happiness to anger as he looked around the room and asked, "Does anyone know how this information got to the public?"

"Ted Maxwell called the police when the man died in the ICU and again when that kid was found dead in the basement," Brian Dawson said, "If the public didn't hear it from him, I bet it came from the police."

"I talked to Ted about both situations, and we concluded that we didn't have much of a choice about calling the police," Mr. Adcock said, "And it's hard for me to believe the information came from the police department because they are so secretive when they're investigating a case."

"Maybe not, but he got a lot of outsiders involved in the hospital's business," he said trying to defend his point of view.

"When it was determined that the man was murdered, it became police business."

"I still think that's how it got out to the public."

"I don't like the fact that it got out, but we might be able to use this to our advantage," Mr. Adcock said, "We may lose a few paying customers, but if it keeps most of the deadbeats away it could be worth it."

"You did say our profit was up," Brian Dawson said with enthusiasm.

"Yes I did, but I still need everyone here to continue to think of ways to save money and increase our profits," Mr. Adcock said, as he got up and walked to the door. "If we do, we may all get a good bonus at the end of the year," and he walked out.

Kelly Adams got up, picked up what papers he had left behind, and followed Larry Adcock out the door.

The hospital department directors sat in silence for several seconds after he left. They looked at each other and smiled.

"That was surprising," Tony Boswell said, "I thought he was going to yell at us, but instead we were given the hopes of a bonus."

"You know he always paints a grim picture to make us

work harder," Hanna Johns said, "Now he's sweetening the situation to encourage us to continue with our efforts."

"Maybe so, but I was starting to worry."

"I was, too."

"I don't know about you guys, but I need to go home so I can come in early tomorrow," Willie Pike said, as he got up and walked out the door.

Everyone else stood up and said, "We do, too," in unison as they left the conference room.

Chapter 29

The Executioner stood in the stairwell watching for an opportunity to go into his target's room. He relished the feeling of adrenalin as it was released into his blood stream, which increased his heart rate and caused euphoria as he accomplished his mission.

He thought back to when he randomly picked victims such as the lady on 3N and, on occasion, would place chemicals in IV fluids as a game of chance to see which patient would fall victim to his endeavors.

Now he had a purpose. A goal with each victim he chose. He was to relieve the hospital of its dead weight. Ease the financial burden that was placed on the institution from patients that didn't have insurance and couldn't pay out of their pocket the cost of services delivered by the hospital. He smiled as he thought of the contribution he was giving to the hospital.

He watched as the nurses finished passing out the nightly meds, making sure to give everything they could to help the patients rest. Then they dimmed the lights after everyone was finished to enhance the desire to sleep.

As the hall darkened, the Executioner watched for several minutes to make sure everyone was settled and no one called out. He reached in his pocket, took out the 10cc syringe filled with regular insulin, and looked to make sure it was still filled to the desired level. After placing it back in his pocket, he carefully eased out of the stairwell into the hall and walked toward his target's door, being very watchful for any potential witnesses as he went.

As he neared the room, he looked at the room number and name tag to verify that it was the person designated to be his next victim. When he was certain he was at the right place, he stood with his ear close to the door for several seconds and listened for any sounds coming from inside. When he didn't hear anything, he slowly inched the door open and stepped inside.

His target was already in a deep sleep with slow shallow breaths.

He carefully closed the door and stood without moving for about a minute to let his eyes adjust to the darkness. Then he took the syringe out of his pocket, eased over to his victim's IV line, and found a port close to the IV pump. He slowly injected the entire 1000 units of regular insulin into his victim's blood stream without disturbing her sleep.

After he emptied the syringe, he moved to the corner of the room to watch his victim die. Within fifteen minutes the insulin started taking affect, and her breathing began to slow. As her sugar dropped, her respirations dropped until she wasn't breathing.

The Executioner moved to the side of the bed and felt for a pulse. When he couldn't find one, he was satisfied she was dead and his job was done. He threw the empty syringe in the sharps container and stepped out into the hall. He looked both ways to make sure he wasn't seen, and then he quickly walked toward the stairs and quietly opened the door.

As the door closed, he took a deep breath to try to slow his heart rate, and then he slowly and confidently walked down the stairs and went out the front door into the parking lot.

Chapter 30

When I got to my office, I found a note taped to my door from Garland Bennett asking me to call him as soon as I could. So I walked to my desk, sat down, and dialed the number to his office.

He answered on the second ring and said, "Garland speaking."

"This is Ted. What can I do for you?"

"A lady died last night on rehab five."

"Do you think she was murdered?"

"I'm not sure, but it seemed suspicious," he said, "She was just sent to rehab yesterday."

"Doctors send patients to rehab all the time that are not truly rehab patients," I said, "Their insurance runs out in the hospital so they send them there to finish their recovery."

"She didn't have insurance," he said, "She was a charity case."

"Oh," I said, as I leaned back in my chair and asked, "How did she die?"

"The nurse said she died in her sleep."

"When did she die?"

"She was discovered at four o'clock this morning when they went to do her vital signs," he said and added, "You know they don't do vital signs every four hours like they do in the hospital because these patients are supposed to be healthy enough for rehab and need their rest more than monitoring."

"Did they code her?"

"It wouldn't have done any good because she had been dead for hours."

"Are you going to do an autopsy?"

"Yes, I talked to the family and persuaded them to allow me to perform an autopsy so we would know how she died."

"When are you going to perform the autopsy?"

"I rushed to get started on it, so I could be through when you called," he said, "I finished it about five minutes ago."

"What did you find?"

"Her blood sugar dropped to almost nothing, which induced a coma and she eventually died."

"Was she a diabetic?"

"No. She had no history of diabetes, and she wasn't on any insulin."

"Did she have a tumor on her pancreas which caused an increase in the production of insulin?"

"There was no sign of a tumor on her pancreas or liver," he said, "All of her organs were fine with only a few changes due to the aging process."

"Then what happened?" I asked, as I took a deep breath, closed my eyes and pleaded, "Don't tell me she was murdered."

"After I did a thorough autopsy and didn't find anything, I turned to the bag of IV fluid and began running tests on it," he said, "The bag contained nothing more than normal saline.

Then I tested the IV tubing and found a large quantity of regular insulin along the lining of the tubing adjacent to the injection port."

"There was insulin inside the IV tubing?"

"Insulin adheres to plastic, so a large portion that's injected into a line will stay inside the line and not enter the blood stream."

"So, are you saying that someone gave her an overdose of insulin?"

"Yes, that's how it appears."

"In your opinion there's no chance it was an accident?" I asked, hoping against hope.

"I wish I could say it was, but with the amount of insulin inside the tubing there must have been several hundred units injected into the line," he said. "There's no way this could be an accident."

"Great!" I quietly swore, and then asked, "What was her name?"

"Her name was Betty Cagle. She was fifty-seven years old and was in the process of recovering from a motor vehicle accident," he said, "She had a right broken femur, her clavicle was broken on her left side, and three ribs that were broken on her left side."

"It sounds like our killer has moved to rehab," I said, as I rubbed my fingers through my hair and added, "This is not good."

"Are you going to call the police?"

"There's really no need because the evidence would be contaminated now, and you've done a thorough autopsy," I said, "I think we might need to send the IV tubing to the CSI lab to be stored with the other evidence."

"I can agree with that," he said, "I've got it in a glass

container right now, and I'll keep it in my office until someone comes by to pick it up."

"I'll call and get someone to pick it up this morning," I said then I placed my phone on the receiver.

I started thumbing through my rolodex until I found the number to the CSI lab. Then I dialed the number and waited while it rang.

The phone was answered on the third ring by a lady with a squeaky voice who said, "CSI office," then she asked, "How may I direct your call?"

"I need to speak to Roger Farris please," I said.

"Who may I say is calling?" she asked.

"Ted Maxwell."

"Just a minute please," she said, as she put me on hold.

I watched the clock as I listened to a well-known rock song being performed in classical music. It had a good sound, but I kept waiting for the drums to kick in to top the song off which never happened.

"Roger speaking," he said, as the music stopped and he answered the phone. "How can I help you Ted?"

"We have some evidence in the morgue at the hospital that I need you to pick up and take to your lab."

"What type of evidence?"

"IV tubing laced with insulin."

"Where did that come from?"

"A lady died this morning and everyone thought it was by natural causes until the autopsy was performed," I explained. "Everything was contaminated except the IV tubing."

"Do you think it was the same killer?"

"Yes, I do."

"Where is the evidence?"

"It is in Garland Bennett's office at the morgue."

"Alright, I'll be there as soon as I can," he said, and my phone went dead.

I placed my phone on the receiver and went to get a cup of coffee.

Chapter 31

I stayed in my office most of the day with my door closed working on my power point presentation on hospital safety. Time was limited because I needed be ready to go to rehab five at shift change to question the staff about the events that happened the previous night.

After finishing my last power point, I hit the save button and turned off my computer. Then I looked at the clock, which indicated it was a quarter after six in the evening. If I hurried I could catch both shifts and possibly question everyone that had been in contact with Betty Cagle, the last victim.

I got up, closed and locked my door, and then I went over the crosswalk leading to the elevators that would take me to rehab five.

When the elevator door opened, I stepped out of the elevator and was standing beside the nurses' desk. I stepped closer and leaned my left arm on the counter top.

As I leaned over the counter toward the lady that was sitting behind the desk, I smiled and asked, "Can I speak to the charge nurse?"

"Which one?" she asked. "Do you want the night shift charge nurse, or the day shift charge nurse?"

"Both," I said. I showed her my badge and added, "I need to speak to everyone that worked today and last night."

She looked at my name badge, then stood up and said, "I'll go get them," and she walked to a group of people standing at the back of the nurses' station.

As she spoke, they turned and looked in my direction.

Then a man in his late forties reluctantly started walking toward me. He held his head down as he approached and didn't look in my direction until he was a few feet away. Then he raised his head and said, "I'm Rick Dunn the night shift charge nurse," and he looked at my name tag. Then he continued, "Amy said you need to speak to us. What's this about?"

"Betty Cagle, the lady that died last night," I said.

"What about her?" he asked.

I looked around the nurses' station and said, "We need to go somewhere else to talk."

"Alright," he said, "We can go to the conference room," and he started walking down the hall.

He stopped at the third door on the right and punched in a code to unlock the door. Then he held it open for me to enter. After I walked inside, he followed me and closed the door.

"Okay, what do you want to know about the woman that died?"

"Did you work last night?"

"Yes, I did."

"Did you have the patient?"

"Yes, she was my patient."

"Why was she getting IV fluids on a rehab floor?"

"She was still getting IV antibiotics, and we always keep patients hooked up to their fluids during the night so we can give them their medicines without waking them up."

"Did you see anyone up here last night that you didn't think belonged?"

"No, I didn't notice anyone," he said and looked at me for a few seconds before asking, "What's this about?"

"I'm just investigating her death."

"I thought she died in her sleep of natural causes."

"I'm just following protocol," I said, as I looked in his eyes and asked, "Is there anything else you can think of that I might need to know?"

"No, I've told you everything I know."

"Alright thanks," I said and looked at the door. "Please send someone else back here, so I can talk to them."

He hesitated before saying, "This is the time we change shifts and people want to give report so they can go home."

"I know, but this is very important and the sooner they come back here the sooner it will be over and they can give report."

"I'll tell them," he said, as he walked out the door.

The next person to walk into the conference room was a lady in her early twenties who didn't hide her agitation with being inconvenienced by having to talk to me.

She huffed as she approached and demanded, "What do you want!"

I smiled which annoyed her even more and asked, "Did you work last night?"

"No, I worked day shift today, and I want to go home."

"Alright, I only have a few questions," I said, "Did you see anyone up here today that you felt didn't belong on the floor?"

"What do you mean?"

"Did someone come to the floor today and ask questions about the lady that died last night?"

"No, you're the first person to come up here and talk about the lady that died," she said, then paused and added, "No, wait a minute. The man from the morgue asked questions when he came to pick up the body."

"Did you see his name tag?"

"He had one on, but I didn't look at it," she said. "I was busy trying to take care of my patients and really didn't care who he was as long as he took the body away."

"Thank you. Please send someone else in."

She turned and walked out the door without saying another word.

The next two people that I talked to worked day shift and had basically the same story as the other lady. They hadn't seen anyone and didn't really care. They just wanted to go home.

The two after that worked night shift, and they backed up the story I had gotten from Rick Dunn. They hadn't seen anyone and they always keep IV fluids attached to the patients when they were receiving antibiotics during the night.

After I finished with the last person, I followed her out of the conference room and went back to the nurses' desk. I looked over the desk at the lady behind the computer and asked, "Did you work last night?"

"Yes, I did," she said.

"Why didn't you come to the conference room so I could talk to you?"

"I thought you only wanted to talk to the nurses."

"No, I wanted to talk to everyone that worked the floor."

"Well than, you also need to talk to Rhonda and Greg."

"Who are they?"

"They're our techs," she said, as she looked behind the desk and added, "Rhonda is dressed in pink scrubs, and Greg is wearing black scrubs."

I looked around the desk to make sure no one could hear, and then I asked, "Did you see anything unusual last night?"

"No, but I stay at the desk all the time."

"No one walked by the desk that you hadn't seen before."

"I honestly don't look at everyone that walks past the desk."

"Alright, can I walk behind the desk and talk to Rhonda?"

"I guess," she said, "You have your badge on, so I guess you can go back there."

I circled around the desk and sat down in a chair beside the lady that had been identified as Rhonda.

She scooted her chair away from me a little, then turned and asked, "Are you the man asking all the questions?"

"Yes, that's me," I said.

"What do you want to know?"

"Did you help take care of the lady that died last night?"

"I was the one that found her dead," she said and shivered, as she remembered. "I grabbed her arm to put the blood pressure cuff on and her arm was ice cold."

"What did you do?"

"I mashed the call button and yelled for Rick to get in there."

"Did you call a code?"

"No, she had already started changing colors," she said and dropped her head as she continued, "Rick said there was no need to call a code."

"What did you do?"

"Rick called the doctor and told him that Mrs. Cagle had

died."

"What did the doctor do?"

"He came down and looked at her," she said, "When he examined the body, he agreed with Rick that they shouldn't call a code. Then he called the family and told them that she had died."

A man wearing black scrubs sat down in a chair beside me and declared, "I worked on the other end of the hall last night, so I don't know anything about the lady that died last night."

I looked at Rhonda who gestured that he was telling the truth.

"Alright, I have one last question then I'll let both of you get to work," I said watching them look intently toward me and asked, "Did either of you see anyone that looked out of place last night?"

"I didn't," Greg said.

"I didn't either," Rhonda said, as she thought for a second and said, "But after we bedded everyone down, we settled in the back and ate. Anyone could have walked up, and we wouldn't have seen them."

"About what time was that?"

"Well, it was after the nurses gave their meds which was somewhere around ten o'clock."

"Did you or the nurse check on the patient after ten o'clock?"

"I generally go into the rooms when they need assistance and the nurse checks on the patient every two hours."

"Did you see Rick check on her?"

"I saw him check on all his patients," she said, "He would crack the door open to see if they were in bed and asleep."

"He didn't go in the rooms?"

"We were told not to disturb them during the hours of ten and four, so they would feel like doing therapy during the day."

"So, you only go into their rooms if they call and ask you to."

"Yes, that is how we do it."

"Thanks for your answers," I said as I got up and walked to the elevator.

When the door opened, I got on the elevator. I hit the button for the first floor and went home.

Chapter 32

I came back to the hospital around midnight and started walking from floor to floor in an attempt to find the killer. It was obvious the killer attacked at night when the patients were sleeping and the hospital staff was less observant of anyone inside the building.

When I got off the elevator on 3N, I slowly started walking toward the nurses' station. Every other light was turned off to save energy and to decrease the light penetrating the rooms. This caused a ghastly shadow to form and contribute to the tension building in my shoulders as I walked up the hall.

The unit was deadly silent as I approached the nurses' station, which caused my footsteps to echo more loudly than they normally would during the day. I slowed my pace in an attempt at lessening the sound of my footsteps as I got close to the nurses' desk.

I eased up to the nurses' station and stopped. I looked at the hospital staff as they continued working on their computers without noticing my presence and thought, 'Anyone could get past them without much effort.'

After several minutes without anyone noticing me, I cleared my throat to get their attention. Everyone instantly stopped working at once and turned in my direction.

Robert Horton stood up and came over to where I was standing. He walked around the counter and whispered, "I didn't hear you walk up."

"I could tell," I said, "I stood there for several minutes without anyone noticing me."

"Is there anything wrong?"

"Everything that's been going on in the hospital has been happening at night, and I want to see if I can do something to change that."

"What do you have in mind?"

"I don't know yet," I said, as I shifted my weight from one leg to the other to decrease the pressure on my lower back then added, "I need to go to the other floors and see if I can form a plan."

Robert looked back at the group of people sitting at the desk and said, "We just finished rounding on our patients, and now it's time to let them sleep a little."

"I have no problem with letting them sleep, but I wonder if someone could be stationed at the end of the hall to watch for any unwanted visitors."

"That wouldn't be a bad idea, but we have to use these computers to chart."

"Is there not a computer on the back hall?"

"There is, but it doesn't work half the time."

I took my note pad out of my shirt pocket and made a note to request the computer on the back hall be fixed before the end of tomorrow. Then I looked down the hall and said, "I'll have it fixed by tomorrow night so someone can sit back there and chart."

"I'm almost finished with my charting for tonight," Robert said. "So, I can go back there and sit when I get finished."

"Until we catch this guy, I would appreciate it if someone would sit back there all the time," I said, as I continued looking at the dimly lit hall.

"It won't take me fifteen minutes, and then I'll go back there," Robert said with assurance.

"Thanks," I said, "Now I need to finish my rounds," and I walked away.

The elevator door was open when I approached, so I jumped on and rode up to the fourth floor. I found exactly the same situation that was on 3N. The halls were dark, and everyone was sitting behind the nurses' desk with their backs toward the entrance.

I walked past the nurses' desk to the back hall and stopped at the computer desk. After quietly pulling the chair out, I sat down and checked the computer to see if it was working. I scanned my emails, surfed the web, and even logged into my restricted website to follow up on some charting that I had been working on earlier.

When I finished, I logged off and went back to the nurses' desk. After standing at the counter for a few seconds without being noticed, I asked, "Can I speak to the person in charge?"

Everyone jumped simultaneously. Bill Franks stood up and slowly walked toward me. He stopped a few feet away and asked, "Can I help you?"

"Yes, you can," I said, "I need someone to sit at the computer in the back and make sure no one walks past the nurses' station without being noticed."

"We'd notice if somebody walked past the nurses' station," he said, as he looked back at the group of people sitting behind the desk.

"Oh, really," I questioned. "Did you notice me when I walked past and sat at the computer for thirty minutes while I checked my email?"

"You...walked past the nurses' station?" Bill asked suspiciously.

"Yes, I did, and I don't believe anybody realized I had."

He looked back at the group of people that had turned completely around and were watching our interaction like they were watching a sporting event. Then he sheepishly turned back to me and said, "I'll sit back there."

He walked to his computer and logged off. Then he grabbed a chair from behind the desk and slowly rolled it down the hall.

I watched him for a while as he walked down the hall then I turned and went back to the elevator. With my two encounters tonight, I realized I needed to have a meeting with the nurse managers to get their involvement in having someone watch the halls during the night. So, I hit the button to the first floor and went home to get some sleep so I could address the issue in the morning.

Chapter 33

As soon as I got to work the next morning, I called Hanna Johns and asked her to arrange a time that I could talk to the nurse managers about the situation that I had encountered the previous night. She informed me that she was having a meeting at ten o'clock with all the nurse managers, and she would give me the last ten minutes to address my concerns at the end of their meeting. She told me to be at the administrative conference room at twenty-five after ten sharp.

I didn't want to be late, so I got to the conference room at a quarter after ten and sat outside the door until it was my time to address the nurse managers.

At exactly twenty-five after ten, the conference door opened. Hanna Johns stuck her head out and said flatly, "You have ten minutes to talk, so get to the point quickly."

I got up, walked into the conference room, and was met with stares from all the nurse managers and an occasional mumble as I walked past on my way to the front of the room. When I reached the podium, the room went quiet and all attention was focused on me.

After one long look around the room, I cleared my throat

and said, "As you all know, we've been having some unfortunate things happen in the hospital lately. I toured the hospital late last night to see if I could come up with some ideas as to what we could do to help prevent this from happening," and I paused and looked at Julie Wells, the nurse manager for 3N, and added, "I went to 3N and watched as everyone worked hard behind the nurses' desk, but no one noticed my presence for several minutes. In fact, if I hadn't made noise to let them know I was there, I could have walked to any patient's room without a single person knowing it."

Then I looked around the room and said, "After that, I went to the fourth floor and walked to the back of the hall without being noticed by the nurses or anyone else at the desk."

"What's your point?" Julie Wells interjected.

"I would like someone stationed in the halls on every floor to make sure no one comes to the floor that doesn't belong."

"How will they get their charting done if they're monitoring the halls?"

"Each floor has a computer on the back hall that can be used for their charting."

"I don't think that computer works on my floor," Mrs. Wells said.

"I'll have it fixed and working wonderfully by the end of the day, or it will be replaced with one that does work."

"You said that my people didn't notice you standing at the nurses' desk," Mrs. Wells questioned, "What were they doing when you were there?"

"They were working on the computers. I assume they were charting, but I couldn't see the computer screens."

"Where was the secretary?" she wondered out loud.

"I presume she was at lunch."

"Oh, I'm sorry. I didn't mean to say that out loud," she said and looked down for a few seconds then she continued, "I'll make sure my floor is covered from now on. I've told them before that someone needed to cover the secretaries when they were at lunch. I specifically addressed this subject in a meeting and designated the nursing assistants to cover the secretary when they were away from the desk."

Elizabeth Pitch spoke up and said, "My people have more important things to do than patrol the halls. The hospital has security personnel hired to walk the halls."

"We have two security officers on duty at night," I said, as I moved around the podium then added, "There is no way they are able to watch the entire hospital at all times."

"There are many things required of our nurses, and I don't want to add anything else on them," she said, glaring at me.

"I'm not asking your nurses to patrol the halls. I just want someone visible in the halls to help decrease the likelihood of another murder occurring."

"You want someone in the halls all night?"

"Yes, they can chart on the computer in the back and watch the back halls while they are charting."

"Time's up," Hanna Johns informed me as she walked toward the podium.

"Just think about. It might save a life on your floor."

"Oh, I've already thought about it, and I'll have it implemented tonight. That is, as long as you get the computer to working," Julie Wells said, as she stood up and said, "I need to go to another meeting," as she walked to the door.

Hanna Johns reached the podium, turned around, and addressed the nurse managers, "I think it's in our best interest to follow the recommendation that Ted has given us. The last thing we want on our floors is another dead body."

"I'll get started on it right now," Julie Wells said, as she walked past me and went out the door.

"Guys, I really just want someone visible on the halls to discourage our killer from striking again," I loudly said as several people walked toward the door in deep conversation with their fellow nurse managers.

Hanna Johns stepped beside me and said, "I'll make sure they understand the importance of having someone stationed on the back hall."

"Thanks," I said, and I walked out the door.

Chapter 34

I could hear my phone ringing when I got to my office door. I quickly unlocked it and rushed inside. I took two long strides, grabbed the phone, and said in a winded voice, "Ted speaking."

"Hey Ted. This is Justin Wells. I thought you might want a report on the evidence we gathered a few days ago."

"Are you talking about the body that was hanging up in the basement?"

"Yes, that's what I'm talking about."

"Sure, I'd like to know what you found."

"There was a trace of blood on the wench that didn't belong to our victim," he said and paused for a few seconds before adding, "The victim was O positive and the blood on the wench was A positive."

"Are you saying our killer is A positive?"

"Yes, that's what I'm saying."

"Can you find our killer from the blood sample?"

"If you find a suspect, I can match his blood with what I have to make a positive identification, but I can't find him by using the blood."

"Well, that's more than we had," I said with enthusiasm.

"That's true," Justin said, "Our killer is getting too confident, and he's starting to leave clues behind."

"Maybe we can catch the killer before he strikes again."

"I hope so."

"Me too," I said and placed the phone on the receiver.

I took my notepad out of my desk and wrote killer at the top of the page. I moved down to the first line and wrote A positive. Then I looked at the almost empty sheet of paper one more time before laying it on top of my desk.

As I leaned back in my chair, I thought about the victims and the way they died. At this point everyone had been killed by a different means. Were they killed by the same person? Was the killer changing his tactics to confuse the police or was he killing people randomly by whatever means he could get his hands on?

Looking over the evidence on my notepad, I realized we only had a blood type that was almost as common as gas stations on the interstate, and the more I stared at it, the more I realized how little we had. So, I put my notepad back in my desk and went to lunch.

Chapter 35

Lunch time, as always, was shorter then I would have liked it to be. But I couldn't keep my mind off the murders that had occurred throughout the hospital, and the idea of a killer walking around the halls scoping out his next victim gave me the motivation to get back to work.

As I sat in the restaurant, I thought of the names of the victims and the floors they were on when they died. Doris Moore was on 3N, John Moss, possibly a failed attempt, was on 4N or MICU, Bert Summerland was on 3N, Rick Sims was on MICU, and Betty Cagle was on the fifth floor in rehab. I didn't place Roy Green in the equation because I didn't know how he fit in the situation. I calculated the probability of which floor the next victim might be on, and according to my calculations based on the pattern the killer seemed to be developing and the fact that the killer seemed to pride himself in his ability to kill wherever he wanted without threat of being caught, I believed the killer would try to rectify his failed attempt and go back to the MICU for his next victim.

So when I walked through the front door, I went straight

to the ICU to see if I could determine which patient might be the next victim. I scanned my badge and walked through the double doors, which are always locked until visiting time.

As the doors closed, I heard someone yell, "Code brown, room 445! I have a code brown, room 445!"

Two nurses got up and walked down the hall toward the room where the man was yelling. They stopped at the door and put on a yellow gown and gloves. Then they went inside.

The aroma drifting up the hall from the room where the two men had entered left no doubt as to what a code brown meant.

A lady pushing a cleaning cart stopped by the door and sprayed room deodorizer in the air and along the baseboard in an attempt at toning down the smell.

I eased up to the nurses' desk and leaned my elbows on the countertop.

"Ted, what are you doing here?" Sonya McGee asked, as she stepped up beside me.

"I have a hunch that I'm trying to follow up on, and I need to talk to one of the nurses about it."

"Alright if you need anything from me just call."

"I will."

She went to the chart rack and put the chart she had in her hands back in its place, then she turned and walked off the floor.

I stayed where I was standing to see how long it would take before anyone noticed me and asked if they could help. It didn't take long before Henry Alexander got up and slowly started walking toward me. I could tell as Henry approached he didn't know whether to be happy to see me or not.

"Is something wrong?" he asked, as he got close.

I put my hand over my mouth and nose to try to repel the

smell that was slowly drifting up to the nurses' desk from the room in the back. "I need to talk to you in private," I said.

"Sure, let's go to the break room, so we can have some privacy and get away from that smell," he said and he walked around the counter toward their break room.

"I heard someone call a code brown when I got to the floor."

"Yeah, I think it's coming from room 445," he said, as he stopped and looked down the hall. "The patient is getting tube fed and hasn't had a bowel movement today until now. He is probably covered from head to toe."

"I remember my days when I worked the floor and the many times I had to clean up a patient who was being fed by a tube."

"Yes, they almost always have diarrhea."

"I know. I guess it's because they're only getting liquids to eat."

"We've been giving him banana flakes, but it doesn't seem to help."

"They may have to change what they are using."

"Yes, they might," he said, as he hurriedly walked toward the break room door and reached his hand toward the doorknob.

I followed without saying another word.

He opened the door and held it for me to walk through.

After the door closed he asked, "What's this about?"

"After much thought, I believe the next victim will be one of the patients on this floor."

"What?"

"I think the killer will strike on this floor."

"Why do you think that?" he asked, as he leaned against the sink.

"Because two people were killed on 3N, one here and one on rehab," I said. "And I just have a gut feeling that the next victim will be on this floor."

"We've had someone at the back computer most of the day," Henry said, "She's not back there now because she is cleaning her patient up and our tech needed some assistance." Then he asked, "Who do you think it will be?" he asked.

"I don't know," I said. "That's why I need to get in their charts to see who has insurance and who doesn't. The killer has been targeting patients without insurance and that will be the probable factor that will determine who he chooses."

"With your job title, I assume you have the right to read anyone's chart as long as it's related to hospital business."

"I do, but I wanted you to know why I was looking at patients' charts."

"I have no problem with you looking at the patients' charts."

"Good, because I want you to go with me and help look through their charts to see if we can determine which patient it will be."

"Shouldn't someone stay in the hall to watch the patients on the back hall?"

"Probably, but I need you with me."

"Alright," he said, as he opened the door and walked out into the hall.

The smell instantly assaulted my nostrils as I stepped out the door. I covered my nose with my hand and rushed to the nurses' desk without speaking.

As we got to the nurses desk, Henry slowed his pace and hesitantly walked toward a group of nurses that was gathered in a corner.

I followed him around the counter and sat down in front

of one of their computers.

Henry leaned over toward the nurses and said, "I am helping Ted with a little research, so we'll be looking through the charts for a little while."

They looked at me, got up, and walked away.

I watched as they left, then I booted up the computer and started looking through the charts for the patients' insurance status.

The first three patients I looked at had insurance from major insurance companies, the next two were listed as having no insurance, and the following four patients had government assisted insurance.

After I finished going down the list, I looked at Henry and asked, "Is this everybody?"

"That's everyone that's on the floor, but there is one in surgery," he said, as he clicked on the recovery page and highlighted one of the patients and added, "This is the guy."

"Click on the patient information page," I said, as I moved toward the computer.

"Oh, here it is," Henry said, "He's a charity case."

"How long has he been here?"

"He's on his third week," he said, as he looked at the admission date. "He has bronchial pneumonia, but the reason he went to surgery was to debride a wound that he has on his sacrum."

"Did he get the wound while he was in the hospital?"

"I'm not sure. Why?"

"If it happened while he was in the hospital, we wouldn't get paid."

"We're not going to get paid anyway," he said and frowned. "He hasn't got any insurance."

"Oh, yeah, I forgot."

"So, who do you think the killer's going to target?"

"I think he'll target one of the three patients without insurance," I replied, as I looked down the patient list then concluded, "I believe the killer will target the guy that had surgery today."

"Why?"

"Because he's been here three weeks already and has the potential to be here a lot longer."

"What are you going to do?"

"I'm not sure right now," I answered, as I stood up and looked around the nurse's desk.

I started to walk off then turned and said, "I need you to make sure someone is at his door tonight, or at least until I come up with a plan to catch this guy."

"If someone's at his door, it might scare the killer off."

"It might, but I don't want anyone else murdered in this hospital. I'll try to have a plan in place by tomorrow night," I said, as I walked away.

Chapter 36

The Executioner, wearing surgery scrubs to disguise himself as a surgeon, slipped through the back door and eased up the stairs. A surgical cap was pulled down over the left side of his forehead in an attempt to cover a scar, which was the result of a motor vehicle accident when he was nine years old.

When he reached the fourth floor, he paused for a few seconds then slowly opened the stairwell door to the ICU and glanced down the hall to see if it was empty.

A lady wearing light blue scrubs was sitting at the computer in the hall. She feverishly worked on the computer with her back toward him and didn't seem to notice the door being opened.

As soon as he saw her, he stopped instantly and remained still for several seconds not knowing what to do. One of his feet was in the hall and the other still in the stairwell. He held his breath as he quietly stepped back into the stairwell, closing the door gently.

He waited a few seconds, and then he opened the door just enough to see if the lady was still sitting at the computer and not alerting others of his presence. When he saw her still working hard at the computer, he breathed a sigh of relief and closed the door without letting it make any noise.

After the door closed tightly, he leaned against the wall and took a few slow breaths as he tried to understand what had occurred. The back halls were always deserted at night, and he could go wherever he wanted without anyone noticing him.

So why was she there? Did they know he took the stairs to reach his targets? Did he leave a clue with the last victim? He smiled confidently as he thought, I'm sure I didn't leave any evidence and they have no clue as to who I am.

Then he closed his eyes which he believed would help him concentrate and tried to think of a good reason for anyone being at the computer. Maybe all the computers at the nurses' desk were occupied. Maybe she wanted to be alone when she charted, or maybe she just wanted to be close to her patients.

He clutched the syringe he had in his shirt pocket and thought, whatever reason she had for being in the hall wouldn't stop his plan but only delay it. It may take him a few days to revise his plan, but his target would be taken out before the end of the week. And if that meant taking out one of the staff members, then so be it. Then he turned and confidently walked down the stairs to the third floor.

When he reached the third floor, he stood in the stairwell and listened for sounds of anyone coming before walking to the first floor. Then he stepped into the lobby and exited out the front door without anyone noticing that he was there.

.

Chapter 37

Duke's House of Gravy was housed in a small run down building at the edge of town. It didn't do much business until the night shift swapped places with day shift. Then it becomes the center attraction, because almost everyone that worked in Westbrook gathered there to eat breakfast. They had seventeen flavors of gravy ranging from the traditional flour based gravy to their most outlandish raspberry gravy and the best buttermilk biscuits that I'd ever eaten.

As I walked in the front door, I stopped at the counter and looked around the dining room until I saw the table where Mark Stone was sitting. He had his back to the wall at a small round table with four chairs in the back corner. Justin Wells was on his right side, and Roger Farris was on his left. I got a cup of coffee from the waitress then walked to the table and sat down in the only chair left.

Mark stopped eating as I approached and asked, "Do you want to eat before we discuss business?"

"Sure," I said, as I sat down. "I can think better on a full stomach."

He nodded and went back to eating.

I looked at Justin who was mixing black pepper gravy with

his eggs.

Roger had biscuits smothered with raspberry gravy.

I turned as the waitress approached with the menu. She smiled and asked, "Do you know what you want, or do you need a menu?"

"I'll have two scrambled eggs, bacon, and a biscuit with black pepper gravy," I said, as I held my coffee cup up and added, "And, a refill of my coffee."

"I'll be right back," she said and smiled, as she hurried away.

We all sat silently as we ate our breakfast.

Mark finished first and sat drinking coffee until everyone had finished. Then he looked at me and asked, "Why did you want us to meet you here?"

I looked around the table then said, "I think I know who the next victim will be at the hospital."

Mark looked at Justin then at Roger and smirked as he asked, "What are you some kind of a psychic?"

"No. I've looked at the pattern that seems to be developing," I said, "He killed two on 3N, then one in the ICU, and one in rehab 5. I think he attempted to kill another patient in MICU but failed. Based on this I believe his next victim will be in the ICU. I think he'll try to make up for his missed attempt."

"Alright, but you said you knew which patient he would kill. There must be at least twelve patients in the ICU on any given day."

Justin looked at Mark then turned to me and asked, "Who do you think he'll kill?"

"Alright guys," I said, "I've looked at all the patients in the ICU, and there are only three that don't have insurance."

"What has that got to do with it?" Justin asked.

I leaned forward and answered, "The killer has only targeted patients without insurance, except for one time, and I believe that was an accident."

"That's still three patients he can choose from," Mark said.

"I know, but I've looked at their length of stay which also is a determining factor, and I think I know which one he'll kill."

"What if you're wrong?" Mark asked.

"I don't know, but it would be unrealistic to think we could have someone in every room," I said, as I looked around the table. "Let's just pray that I'm right."

"Alright, what is your plan?" Mark asked.

I leaned over the table and whispered what I thought was a very detailed plan as to how we could catch the killer.

Mark interjected a few pointers to enhance the plan and simplify the main objective.

Justin and Roger added a few items to the plan.

After a lot of discussion, we came to an agreement as to how the plan should be set up. We decided to put it in action tonight and hopefully catch the killer before anyone else got hurt.

"Well, if nothing happens I'll see you at the hospital tonight," I said, as I got up, shook their hands and walked out the door.

Chapter 38

Hanna Johns met me at the door when I got to the hospital and announced, "We have a problem."

"What kind of a problem do we have?" I asked while trying to sound concerned.

"Crystal City Accreditation Service is making a surprise visit today, and we still have that murderer running loose in the hospital."

"If it's a surprise visit, then how do you know they're coming today?"

"They always send us an email the morning before they get here to let us know that they are coming," she said, as she grabbed my arm and pulled me toward the edge of the lobby and asked in a low voice, "How close are you to finding the killer?"

"I'm not sure," I said as I scanned the lobby for anyone that might be a little too interested in what we were saying. After I didn't see anyone, I continued, "We're still compiling the evidence we have, but at this point we still haven't identified the killer."

"This killer has really caused the hospital some valuable

business," she said.

"And potentially a very large law suit," I added.

"That's true," she said, as she looked at me and asked, "Is it that hard to find the killer?"

"It is when there are no clues."

"I thought the police gathered evidence the other night."

"They did."

"Then why can't they use their evidence to catch the killer?"

"The killer didn't leave much evidence," I said as I lowered my voice and continued, "This isn't like the television crime shows. He was very careful and didn't leave anything to be used to identify him."

"I didn't say it was," she said a little perturbed. "I just need this to be over with."

"I'm doing…," I said and stopped as a man in his fifties walked by pushing a wheelchair with a lady in her eighties to the elevator. I watched and waited until they were far enough away to not be able to hear, then I said, "I'm doing the best I can."

She followed my gaze and said, "I know, but it would be best if….," and then she stopped talking as she looked at the door where two men dressed in matching three piece gray suits and a lady wearing a light gray jacket and slacks casually walked into the lobby.

They stood at the door for several seconds then proceeded to walk to a group of chairs at the edge of the lobby and sat down.

"They're here," Hanna Johns said, "I've got to go," and she rushed over to where they were sitting.

I watched as she quickly walked over and greeted them with a large smile and handshake. Then I turned and went to my office to decide whether to go through with the plan tonight or postpone it until the Crystal City Accreditation Service completed their evaluation of the hospital.

Chapter 39

When I put the key in my office door, I heard my phone start ringing. I quickly unlocked the door and rushed to the phone. At the end of the third ring I picked it up and said, "Ted speaking. How can I help you?"

"Ted, this is Henry Alexander," a male voice said.

"Oh, hello Henry," I said, "How can I help you?"

"You know that guy we were talking about yesterday that had surgery."

"Yes. What about him?"

"You won't have to worry about someone murdering him because he just died."

"What?"

"That man that you thought the killer would target, because he didn't have insurance, just died."

"How did he die?"

"You know I told you he was in the ICU because of a respiratory infection."

"Yes, I remember that."

"Well, after surgery he went into respiratory distress and never recovered."

"I thought he was on a ventilator?" I asked, as I leaned my elbow on top of my desk.

"He was, but he pulled his endotracheal tube out of his mouth and died before we were able to re-intubate him."

"Are you sure he pulled the tube out?"

"Yes, I'm sure," Henry said, "It was witnessed."

"Well, that answers one of the questions I was trying to answer."

"What's that?"

"Oh, nothing," I said, "Just something I was thinking about."

"Is there anything special you want done with the body?" Henry asked.

"No, I don't think so," I said, "Just send it to the morgue, and we'll let Garland Bennett decide if an autopsy should be done."

"Alright, I'll call the morgue attendant to pick up the body."

"Henry, thanks for letting me know," I said, and I placed the phone back on the receiver.

I sat at my desk trying to decide what to do next. Should we pick another patient and try to set a trap to catch the killer or should we cancel it for now? As I thought, I sat with my elbows on the desk and my hands resting on either side of my face while I tried to think through the events that had occurred earlier today.

After several minutes of fluctuating between whether to go ahead with the plan by using another patient or regrouping and trying it another day, I picked up my phone and called Mark Stone to inform him of the situation. After a long discussion, we decided to cancel the plans we had concocted at breakfast and arranged another meeting the following morning to come up with a plan to apprehend the killer.

Chapter 40

The Executioner stood at the stairwell with his hand firmly gripping the door handle and watching Susan Brunner as she charted on the computer. After a few seconds, he slowly closed the door making sure not to make any noise as it met the doorframe. He decided to wait until everyone was finished giving their medications and the halls were deserted before making his move toward his target.

As he thought through his plan, he smiled a little half smile. He clutched his handkerchief and the bottle of chloroform that he intended to use to get past his one obstacle between him and the target.

The Executioner prided himself in his ability to adapt. He met his many challenges by being creative. He had made his own chloroform by mixing acetone with sodium hypochlorite and removing the byproduct, which is chloroform by distillation.

He thought back to the many hours he had spent in the chemistry lab learning to mix different chemicals together and studying their reactions. At the time he only believed he was doing it to get through school, but he enjoyed every minute of it and remembered most everything he learned. His instructor was fond of saying that someday we might be able to use what we had learned. Today was that day.

He looked at his watch, which indicated it was five after eleven at night. All the medicines would be given and everyone would be settled in front of their computer charting for the night.

So, he took the door handle and slowly turned it to the left. After a count of three, he inched the door open and glanced out toward the computer to see if anyone was sitting in his path. As before Susan Brunner was in front of the computer with her back facing the stairwell door.

Before stepping out into the hall, he looked in both directions to make sure the hall was empty. Then he looked back at Susan and thought, casualties were something he had considered before he started the mission. Susan Brunner was going to be one of the unfortunate ones that got in his way.

As he stepped out of the stairwell into the hall, he readied his handkerchief and the bottle of chloroform. He loosened the top of the bottle but kept it covered to contain the smell. Then he quickly stepped toward Susan Brunner. The closer he got the more tense he got because he thought she would turn around at any moment.

When he got within five feet of her, he took the top off the bottle of chloroform and poured a generous amount into the handkerchief. Then he cupped it over her nose and mouth. He held it tight until she quit struggling and became motionless.

As her body went limp, he pulled her out of the chair and carried her to the closest room without a patient, the room beside the stairs, and dropped her on the bed.

The Executioner tied a tourniquet around her arm, and

then he took a syringe out of his pants pocket and started examining the veins on her arms. As the veins appeared he chose a large one in her left antecubital fossa and shot the contents of the syringe into her vein.

As the drug circulated through her system, her body relaxed even more and her respirations declined until she wasn't breathing at all.

After taking a couple steps back, he looked down at her lifeless body and said, "Thirty milligrams of morphine was probably a little overkill, but I wanted to make sure you didn't suffer," then he walked out the door and confidently walked to his target's room.

He reached the door in less than a minute and glanced up the hall toward the nurses' station to make sure no one had noticed him. Then he walked inside.

The target was lying flat on his back while a dim light was shining under the bed.

The Executioner blinked his eyes several times to adjust his vision to the darkness, and then he carefully moved to the foot of the bed.

The target didn't move.

The killer looked at his target's face, which had a large mask covering his nose and mouth and a thin plastic line leading to the wall. He then scanned the room to get an idea of the equipment that was being used to keep his target alive.

Not being able to see very well from where he was standing, he stepped around the bed and noticed a large four channel IV pump with several drugs infusing through a quad lumen central line. One line had normal saline with Vancomycin piggy- backed through a port at the top of the tubing. Another line had heparin sodium infusing at 12 cc an hour. The third line had TPN infusing at 62.6 cc an hour. The fourth line was open for blood draws or IV push meds.

As the Executioner calculated the cost of what was hanging he shook his head and mumbled, "The TPN cost about a thousand dollars a bag alone," then he stepped close to his target and reached for the line that was used for IV push.

He paused as the target opened his eyes and looked questioningly at him. Then he stepped closer to him.

"Why are you here?" the target mumbled through the mask that was covering his face.

"What?" the Executioner asked just to see if he would repeat himself.

The target feebly lifted his left hand and pulled the mask to the side of his face. "Why are you here?" he asked, as he labored to breath.

The lone figure smiled and said, "I have a little something to help you sleep."

The target smiled and said, "Good. I need whatever I can, to help me get some rest," then he put the mask back over his nose and mouth and closed his eyes.

"You should be sleeping in a few minutes," he said, as he took a syringe out of his pocket and pushed 200 milliequivalent of potassium chloride through the open port.

The target's eyes popped open, and he grasped the bedrails with both of his hands. His body jerked a couple of times as if he was having a seizure, and then he slumped over in the bed and remained motionless with his eyes wide open.

The Executioner left the room and slipped down the hall toward the stairs as the monitors began to alarm. He looked up and down the hall making sure no one had seen him. Then he quietly opened the door and went down the stairs.

Chapter 41

I rolled over and looked at the clock as my phone started ringing. According to the large red numbers it was one forty-five in the morning, and all I could think was oh my God, not another dead body.

After the third ring, I hesitantly picked the phone up and said in a scratchy voice, "Ted speaking."

"The killer has struck again," Sonya McGee said without introducing herself. "And this time he killed a nurse in the process."

"Who's speaking?" I asked.

"I'm sorry," she said, "This is Sonya McGee. I'm so upset about the murders that I forgot to identify myself."

"That's alright," I said, as I instantly woke up and asked, "Who was killed?"

"The nurse that was killed was Susan Brunner," she said, "And the patient was Tim Sanders."

"What room was he in?"

"416 I think," she said then added, "He was moved there from the floor yesterday."

"Alright, have someone put on a pot of coffee, and I'll be

there as soon as I can," I said, as I placed the phone on the receiver and sat up on the side of the bed.

"What's wrong?" Sara asked in a sleepy voice.

"I've got to go to the hospital," I said, "There's been another murder."

"Be careful," she said as she rolled over and put her hand on my shoulder. "Ted, I love you, and we need you to stay safe."

"I know, and I'll be as careful as I can," I said as I gently kissed her on the lips. "Honey, go back to sleep. I'll see you when I get home tonight."

"Alright," she said as she turned over, fluffed her pillow, and closed her eyes.

After stretching my neck to remove the tension, I got up and walked into the bathroom. I turned the water on to take a shower. Then I turned it off as I realized I needed to call Mark Stone and have him meet me at the hospital. So, I walked back into my bedroom and punched in his cell phone number.

His phone rang several times before a sleepy voice answered, "Mark speaking," and then he said, "This better be important."

"Mark, this is Ted," I said, "I need you to meet me at the hospital."

"Why?" he asked. "It's two o'clock in the morning."

"There's been another murder," I said, "And this time he killed a nurse along with the patient."

"Two people were killed?"

"Yes."

"I'll be there as fast as I can," he said.

"Mark, wait," I yelled.

"What?"

"I need you to call Justin and Roger and have the CSI unit meet us at the hospital to investigate the murders."

"No problem," he said. Then my phone went dead.

I laid my phone on the receiver and went into the bathroom to take a shower. After I showered, I put on a pair of light brown dress pants, a maroon dress shirt, and dark brown dress shoes. Then I rushed out of the house, got in the car, and drove to the hospital.

Chapter 42

The ICU looked like a convention of hospital directors. Tony Boswell, director over rehab services, and Brian Dawson, director over surgery, were standing by the nurses' desk talking to Elizabeth Pitch, nurse manager of the ICU. Hanna Johns, the hospital's CNO, was standing in the hall talking to Doctor Sonya McGee. Garland Bennett, the hospital's pathologist, and Doctor Willie Pike, the hospital's chief of staff, were standing in front of one of the rooms in deep discussion.

Hanna Johns was the first to notice me. She stopped talking almost immediately and slowly walked in my direction. We met before I reached the nurses' desk.

There was no smile on her face. In fact, she looked highly stressed. She hadn't taken the time to apply makeup or dress in her usual attire. She was wearing a pair of faded blue jeans and a navy blue button front oversized shirt. On her feet she wore a pair of flip flops that one would wear around the house for convenience.

When she got to me, she took a deep breath and collapsed against the wall. She focused her eyes toward the ceiling and said tearfully, "I shouldn't have gotten in your way. I should have let you go through with your plan to catch the killer."

"You didn't talk me out of anything," I said, "The patient that I thought the killer was going to target died early in the day. That's why I didn't go ahead with the plan."

"But I asked you to wait until the Crystal City Accreditation Service completed their survey."

"I know, but my main objective was to catch the killer and at this point that meant not listening to you."

Hanna Johns looked me in the face without smiling. Her whole demeanor changed and she asked, "You do know I'm the CNO of the hospital?"

"Yes, I do. But I also know that Larry Adcock is the CEO of the hospital, and he told me to do whatever it took to catch the killer."

"If you had a higher education, you'd know the chain of command and understand that I could have your job in a heartbeat for insubordination."

I moved a little closer to her and whispered, "If you read my job description, you'd know that it specifically states that the only person who can fire me is the CEO of the hospital," and I took a step closer and added, "It was written that way to decrease the amount of threats I'd get when I was trying to do my job."

She stood speechless for a few seconds, but then she walked away.

I watched her as she walked back to the nurses' desk and disappeared around the corner. Then I eased past and went down the hall to where Garland Bennett and Willie Pike were talking.

They turned as I approached, but continued with their conversation.

"What did you say?" I asked as I stepped up beside them catching the last part of what Garland Bennett was saying.

"Oh, I was just saying that the killer must have entered the floor from the stairwell."

"Why do you think that?" I asked.

"Because the evidence shows that Susan Brunner was at the computer and the killer brought her to the closest room to dispose of her."

"What evidence?"

"She was still signed in on the computer," Dr. Bennett said, as he pointed to the desk computer and the chair that was turned onto its side. Then he pointed to a room beside the stairwell and added, "And her body was found in that room which was the closest room to the computer."

"You didn't touch anything?" I asked as I looked down the hall at Mark Stone and the CSI team as they hurried toward us.

"Lord, no," he said indignantly. "I know enough about crime investigation to know not to touch anything that might be considered evidence."

"I'm sorry," I said, "I didn't mean to offend you."

"That's alright," he said, looking a little embarrassed. "I guess it's a little too early in the morning, and I didn't get much sleep last night. I usually don't wear my feelings on my sleeve like I seem to be doing this morning."

"That's alright. We're all a little tense right now."

"Where was the victim killed?" Roger Farris asked as soon as he got beside me.

I looked at Garland Bennett.

He looked at Willie Pike and said, "He got here first, so I'll let him tell you what he saw."

"The person that I believe to be the first victim is Susan

Brunner, and her body is in the room beside the stairwell. The second victim, who I believe to be the one that the killer was targeting, is in this room," Willie Pike said, as he pointed to the room they were standing in front of.

"I'll take this room, and you take the other one," Roger said, as he picked up his evidence bag and walked into the victim's room.

I watched as he took a camera out of his bag and started photographing the room.

Justin Wells didn't say anything. He just picked up his evidence bag and walked into the room where Susan Brunner's body was lying.

Mark Stone followed Roger to the door and looked inside at the victim. Then he turned around and asked, "Who found the bodies?"

"Sonya McGee called me," I said, "She's one of the doctors on this floor."

"Hanna Johns called me," Willie Pike said.

"Hanna Johns is the one that called me, too," Garland announced with surprise then he questioned, "I wonder if that's who called the rest of the directors?"

"That's a good question," Mark said, "But I want to know the name of the first person that saw the victims after they were killed."

"Maybe we should ask Dr. McGee," I said, "I think she called me as soon as she pronounced the victims dead."

"Or, right after she called Hanna Johns," Mark said and smiled.

"Or maybe right after she called Hanna Johns," I agreed and started walking toward the nurse's desk.

The first person I saw when we got to the nurses' desk was Hanna Johns who turned swiftly around and walked into the back.

"That was odd," Mark said.

"I think she's a little perturbed at me right now," I said.

"Really," he said with a quizzical look on his face. Then he looked toward me and asked, "What'd you do?"

"I'll tell you about it later," I said, "We have something that's more important to do right now."

"I know, but I thought we could talk while we looked for the potential witness."

"I don't want to talk about it now."

"Alright," he said, "It's up to you."

"I don't see Sonya McGee, but there's Elizabeth Pitch, the floor's nurse manager," I said, as I started walking toward her. "Maybe she can tell us who found the bodies."

She frowned as we approached and hesitated a few seconds before she broke away from Brian Dawson and Tony Boswell, who she was still standing beside, and started walking toward us.

Brian took a few steps with her, but stopped as Tony grabbed his arm and whispered something into his ear.

He looked at us, gave us an acknowledging nod, and then walked with Tony to the back of the nurses' station.

Elizabeth Pitch met us halfway. She looked at Mark then at me and announced, "I think this might be the worst day of my career."

"I can truly say that the last three months have been the worst that I have experienced since I started working in the hospital setting," I said as I took her arm and led her to the side of the nurses' station where no one could overhear what we were saying.

After we got away from everyone, I asked, "Do you know who discovered the bodies?"

She arched her brow and looked at Mark without answering.

"Oh, I'm sorry," I said, "This is Mark Stone with the police department."

He stuck his hand out and said, "I'm sorry we had to meet under these circumstances."

She shook his hand and said, "Yes, it would have been better to have met another way," then asked, "Now, what were you asking?" as she looked back at me.

"Who found the bodies?" I asked.

"Helen Wade found Susan Brunner's body after we coded Mr. Sanders," she said. She looked around to see if Helen was at the desk, so she could point her out to us. When she didn't see her, she continued, "Susan was Mr. Sanders' primary nurse. When he coded, no one knew where Susan was, so Helen went looking for her. Christy Mann was the main nurse working on Mr. Sanders' code."

"I need to speak to both of them," Mark said, as he looked across the nurses' station.

"I know, but I don't know where they are right now," she said irritably, as she followed his gaze.

"Where do you think they might be?" he asked.

"They do have their own patients to take care of," she said, as she started to defend them. "I would imagine they are in their patients' rooms, either drawing labs or giving medicines."

"Do you have anyone that can watch their patients while I talk to each nurse?"

"Let me see," she said, "I'll need to check with the charge nurse for a minute, but I think I can get her to watch the patients long enough for you to talk to them," and she walked away.

"I thought you said she was the nurse manager," Mark said after she was gone.

"I did."

"Then why does she have to ask the charge nurse to see if she can watch the patients."

"I don't know."

"All the bosses I ever had told me what to do."

"Me, too," and I sat down in one of the chairs to wait for Elizabeth to return with one of the nurses.

Chapter 43

In about ten minutes, Elizabeth Pitch returned followed by a lady in her early fifties with light brown hair with scattered patches of gray. She was wearing a pair of bright pink scrubs with matching pink shoes.

The lady looked uncomfortable as she approached, but tried to hide it with a strained smile.

Mark and I stood up as soon as we saw them coming and we slowly started walking in their direction.

We met them as they reached the corner of the nurses' desk.

They stopped and waited for us to begin our questions.

"I'm sorry," I said, "But I think we should talk to Ms. Wade somewhere that's a little more private."

Elizabeth looked around the empty desk. She pointed and declared, "There's nobody here."

"I know, but someone might walk up while we are talking, and I don't want to be interrupted."

"I guess you can go to the break room," she said, as she let out a sigh of exasperation.

"That would be great," I said and smiled.

"Alright, let's go," she said, as she started walking down the hall toward the break room.

She punched in the code, opened the door and held it until everyone was inside. Then she looked at me and said, "This is Helen Wade. She found Susan Brunner's body."

I turned and looked at the lady as she let out a small compressed sound that could have been her fighting back tears.

She lowered her head and looked away.

"Call me when you're finished talking to Helen, and I'll go get Christy Mann so you can talk to her," Elizabeth Pitch said, as she stepped out in the hall and closed the door behind her.

After the door closed, Mark turned his full attention to the lady and asked, "What is your name?"

She looked puzzled.

"Mrs. Pitch just told you my name," she said as she gave me a questioning look.

"I know, but I need you to tell me so I can put it on the record."

"Alright," she said and frowned. "My name is Helen Wade."

"How long have you been a nurse?"

"Six years."

"How long have you worked on this floor?"

"Six years," she said and smiled. "This is the only place I've worked," then she added, "I mean this is the only place I've worked as a nurse."

"What did you do before you became a nurse?"

"I don't see what this has to do with me finding Susan Brunner's body," she responded, as she stood up and went to the coffee pot.

"I'm just trying to get a little background before I start the interview," Mark said in a calm voice. "I didn't mean to upset you."

She poured a cup of coffee and sat down without saying anything.

"I was married for twenty years and stayed at home with my children," she said as she stared into nothingness. "Then my husband died, and I had to get a job. So, to answer your question, I guess you can say I was a housewife before I went into nursing."

"I'm sorry," he said, "I didn't mean to pry. It's just protocol to get a little history before we start our questioning."

"That's fine. It's not something I'm trying to hide," she said. "It brings back sad memories, but I know it's something I have to deal with."

"What did you do when you found Susan Brunner's body?"

"What do you think I did?" she asked. "I yelled for help."

"Did you go in the room to make sure she was dead first?"

"Actually, when I saw the tourniquet close to her arm I thought she might have shot up some drugs and maybe overdosed."

"Did she have a problem with drugs?"

"Not that I'm aware of, but sometimes people hide it well."

"That's true," he said in agreement then asked, "Did you go in the room before you called for help?"

"Yes. I checked to see if she had a pulse," she said as she dropped her head and remained quiet as she remembered finding Susan Brunner's body.

"Then what did you do?"

"I stuck my head out the door and called for help. Then I went back and started CPR."

I got up and went to the coffee pot. After pouring two cups of coffee, I placed one cup in front of Mark and sat down with the other cup in my hand.

They stopped talking and watched me until I stopped moving then Mark asked, "Did you see anyone on the floor that didn't belong?"

"No, I didn't see anyone, but I'm usually too involved with my patients to notice anything," she said, "I have had people walk by me without me seeing them. Let me explain that," and she looked at me and added, "I'm usually focused on the next task that I need to do, and therefore I don't notice my entire surroundings."

"So if the killer walked past the nurses' desk and you were standing there, you might not have noticed him."

"That's possible, but she was in the back hall all night," she said defensively. "She stayed at the computer in the back."

Mark looked at me.

"That was one of the things I asked each floor to do in an effort to keep the killer from coming on the floor," I said.

"It didn't work," Mark said, stating the obvious.

"I know."

"So, you're the reason she was on the back hall by herself," Helen Wade said, as her voice began to rise. "She didn't have anyone to watch her back."

"This is not the time for placing blame," Mark interrupted. "We need to focus on the circumstances of Ms. Brunner's death."

"She's dead," she said and a tear ran down her face. "And she wouldn't have been back there if he hadn't told the nurse manager to have someone sit on the back hall."

"Don't you think that's crossed my mind," I said, defensively.

"She was murdered," she said, as she burst into tears.

"I know, and it's our job to find her killer," Mark said.

"That won't bring Susan back!" she said, as she sniffed.

"True, but it might stop anyone else from being killed," Mark said, as he looked Helen Wade in the face.

"If I had seen something, I'd tell you," she said softly.

"Tell me about Susan Brunner's patient, Mr. Sanders."

"His monitor was showing rhythm changes. Susan wasn't at the desk, so Christy went into the room to check on him. She was the one who called the code. The doctor was asking questions about the patient's history and care, some we couldn't answer. Susan didn't show up for the code, so the charge nurse sent me to look for her," Helen said with a look of pain on her face.

Mark looked at Helen quietly for a moment then handed her his card and said, "I don't have any more questions, but if you think of anything else, give me a call," as he pushed back his chair and stood up.

"I'm sorry I didn't see anything," she apologized.

"That's alright," I said, as I stood up and opened the door. "Just tell Elizabeth Pitch that we're ready to talk to Christy Mann."

"Alright, I'll let her know," she said, as she walked out the door.

After the door closed, we got another cup of coffee and went back to the table to wait for the next person we needed to interview.

Chapter 44

Mark and I looked at the door simultaneously as it opened and a lady in her mid-twenties walked inside the break room.

She smiled nervously as the door closed.

I stood up and said, "My name is Ted Maxwell with patient safety in the hospital."

She said, "I'm Christy Mann."

I pointed to Mark and said, "This is Mark Stone with the police department."

Mark stuck his hand out and said, "Ms. Mann, please have a seat."

She shook his hand without saying anything and sat down across from him.

"I have a few questions I need to ask you about the murders tonight," Mark said.

"Like what?"

"Did you see anyone in the hall that you didn't think belonged?"

"To tell you the truth, I didn't see anybody in the hall."

"No family members or anyone?"

"Visiting hours are over at nine o'clock, and Susan

Brunner was still alive at that time because I saw her giving medications to her patients."

"Is that the last time you saw her alive?"

"Yes, but she was on the back hall, and I was in the front," she said, "I couldn't see her from where I was."

"What was going on with Tim Sanders when you went into his room?"

"When I walked in, he was clutching his chest and his face was contorted with pain. By the time I had pushed the button to call a code, he had flat- lined," she stated with a loud sigh.

"What happened after that?"

"The doctor was asking questions about Mr. Sanders that I wasn't able to fully answer since I wasn't his primary nurse. We asked everyone that came into the room if they had seen Susan. No one had, so the charge nurse sent Helen to look for her."

"What happened then?"

"Helen found Susan in one of the back rooms and called a code."

"What about Mr. Sanders? What happened next with him?"

"We continued doing CPR, after almost an hour, the doctor called time of death."

"Who pronounced him dead?"

"Dr. McGee."

I interrupted and asked, "Do you think the code was run proficiently?"

"I think so," she said. "Why?"

"I was just making sure we did everything we could to save him."

"We ran a full code," she said with certainty. "There was nothing else we could have done to save him."

"Did you touch anything when you went into the room?"

"I only touched his carotid artery to check for a pulse, but I'm sure a lot of other stuff was touched when we were running the code."

Mark looked at me and said, "We'll need to get fingerprints from everyone on the floor."

I started to respond, but stopped when I heard a light knock on the door.

Justin was looking through the small glass window as he gently pecked with the knuckle of his ring finger against the side of the glass.

"Let me see what he wants," I said, as I got up and opened the door.

"I've finished gathering evidence in the room where Susan Brunner's body was located," Justin said, "Glen Watts is loading the body on a stretcher to take it back to the forensic lab for an autopsy."

"Glen Watts," I said, as I looked at Mark and asked, "Did you call him?"

"Yes, I did," he admitted. "This case has become too involved to keep it contained inside the hospital. I know Garland Bennett is a good pathologist, but this case is more complex than we once thought. I think we need a forensic pathologist to determine the cause of death."

"You do know he trained Glen Watts," I retorted.

"I know Glen began his training with Garland Bennett, but he finished his training at the police department under the supervision of Walter Franks, one of the best known forensic pathologists in Oregon," Mark defended.

Christy Mann looked at Mark, turned to me, and asked, "Are you finished with me?"

"No," I said, "I want Justin to get your fingerprints before you leave the break room."

"What?" Justin asked.

"I need you and Roger to fingerprint everyone on the floor," I said, "And I'd like you to set up in here."

"Alright, I can do that," Justin said, as he walked to the table and sat his evidence bag down.

He pulled out a container and began putting everything he needed to begin the fingerprinting process on the table and in the precise order he would need them.

Christy sat down to wait and crossed her legs as she watched Justin.

"I'll check on Roger and have him start fingerprinting people if he's through gathering evidence," Mark said, as he walked to the door and opened it.

I followed Mark out the door to let Justin get started without me hovering around.

As Mark turned to walk to the victim's room, I said, "I'll get people lined up to be fingerprinted," and I walked up the hall.

Elizabeth Pitch met me when I got to the nurses' desk with her hands on her hips. "Are you and your friends finished disrupting my floor," she demanded, as her head began bobbing from side to side.

"We need to fingerprint everyone that went into the victims' rooms," I said in a calm voice.

"Well, how long is that going to take?" she asked in an irritated voice.

"It depends on how long it takes you to round them up so they can be fingerprinted," I responded without hesitation.

"So, it's my job to round them up," she said.

"It would help us get things done more quickly."

"Where do I need to get them to wait?"

"They've started fingerprinting in the break room, so I guess you can have them wait up here and we'll call them when it's their turn."

"Alright, let's get started," she said, as she walked to the back of the nurses' desk and yelled, "Anybody that went into the rooms where Susan Brunner and Tim Sanders were killed must come to the front of the nurses' desk and wait to be fingerprinted!"

"Where do you want Roger to setup?" Mark asked, as he walked up the hall with Roger following close behind.

"That's a good question," I said, as I looked around the nurse's desk. "Why don't you set up beside the printer."

"I'm not sure there's enough room by the printer," Roger said, as he walked around the nurses' desk and looked at the counter space. He slid the printer over a few inches and said, "It'll be tight, but I think I can make it work."

I turned to one of the nurses, waiting to be fingerprinted, and said, "You'll be first," then I looked at the rest and said, "Form a line behind her."

Christy Mann stopped at the edge of the nurses' desk and announced, "He's finished with me. Someone else needs to go to the break room to be fingerprinted."

A man in his late forties with short black hair jumped at the opportunity. He rushed around the counter and went down the hall toward the break room.

Sonya McGee stepped up beside me and said, "I heard you wanted to fingerprint everyone that entered the victim's rooms."

"We need to," I responded.

"I think you already have my fingerprints on file," she said. "Do you still need to fingerprint me tonight?"

"I think it would be best to do everyone just to make sure

we have everything we need."

"That's fine," she said, "I walked over here with Chester West, the resident who ran the code on the nurse, so I might as well get fingerprinted myself."

"Thanks," I said.

"I don't want any confusion," she said, as she got in the back of the line.

I went around the counter and stood with Mark while we waited.

I glanced at Garland Bennett who was walking behind Glen Watts as he pushed the stretcher with the body of Tim Sanders past the nurses' desk.

Garland smiled but didn't say anything as they went down the hall.

"Hey, Ted, can we talk to you a minute?" Brian Dawson asked, as he and Tony Boswell emerged from behind the nurse's desk.

I looked at Mark who was casually observing everyone at the desk as he relaxed with his back against the wall and his arms loosely crossed. He didn't say anything but glanced in their direction.

"Sure, I guess," I said, as I stepped toward them.

They walked about ten feet from the nurses' desk and stopped.

"What do you want?" I asked when I reached them.

"How is the investigation going?" Tony Boswell asked.

"That's between me and the police."

"Now, we're just trying to help," Tony said.

"How do you think you're going to help?"

"I don't know, but if we knew how the investigation was going, we might know how we could help."

"Do you know who the killer is?"

"No."

"Then you don't have any information for me."

"You don't have to get smart," Brian Dawson said, as he stepped toward me.

"And you don't have to interrogate me," I responded, "The murders are being investigated by the police department, and they have all of the information. If you really want to know how the investigation is going then go ask Mark Stone. See if he'll tell you anything."

Justin and Roger walked past us carrying their evidence gathering equipment and went to the elevator.

Mark hesitated at the nurses' desk for a few seconds before walking to where we were standing.

"Well, we need to be going," Brian said, as soon as Mark stopped.

"Yes, we need to leave," Tony agreed, and they walked away.

"I took a bath this morning," Mark said and laughed.

"They were trying to see what information they could get out of me," I said.

"I didn't mean to run them off."

"That's fine," I said, "I wasn't going to tell them anything."

"The less information we let out, the better off we'll be."

"I agree."

"I'll call you later on today if anything develops from the evidence the CSI guys gathered," Mark said.

"What about the meeting we were supposed to have this morning?" I asked in a low voice.

"Let's change the time to three o'clock this afternoon," Mark said. "Maybe by then we'll have a little more information on which to base our decision."

"I have ideas, but I think if we brainstorm we'll have a better chance of catching this guy."

"I'll see you at three," Mark said and then he walked to the elevator.

After Mark got on the elevator, I went back to the nurses' desk and asked, "Is Hanna Johns still here?"

Helen Wade glanced up from her computer and said, "No, she left about an hour ago when you were in the break room talking to Christy."

"Thanks," I said. Then I walked off the floor.

Chapter 45

When I got to my office, I booted up my computer and looked into the financial status of our latest victim. Just as I thought, he had no insurance and had the potential for being in the hospital for several weeks.

I got my notepad out of my desk drawer, wrote Tim Sanders under the ICU category, and then I looked at the rest of the names to familiarize myself with the other victims.

All but one of the victims didn't have insurance and the majority of the victims were likely to be in the hospital for several days to weeks.

At the top of my list were the victims on 3N. It appeared that Bert Summerland's death was randomized, and no one in particular was targeted. He had insurance and was likely going home the next day.

Doris Moore, however, seemed to have been targeted because of her physical condition and the fact that she didn't have insurance. It may have been a mercy killing because of her stage four cancer, but with the other victims being killed, more likely she was murdered in order to decrease the cost to the hospital.

The next patient to be killed was Rick Sims in the ICU. Just like Doris Moore, he didn't have insurance, but did potentially have several more weeks to stay in the hospital. Another patient killed to save money.

Betty Cagle was killed in rehab 5. She fit the same description as the other victims. No insurance and a long stay in the hospital.

As I looked down the list, the two factors that kept screaming out at me were the fact that every victim except one was a financial drain on the hospital and they were likely to be in the hospital for several weeks.

I sat back in my chair as the realization that the hospital might be involved in the murders suddenly dawned on me.

Was that the reason all the directors showed up in the ICU?

They pretended to be concerned with the death of a hospital employee, but were they attempting to tamper with evidence to conceal the killer's identity or just watching to see what we found in the investigation?

As I looked back at the behavior of the directors during the night, I remembered the frustration Hanna Johns showed when I got the police involved in the murders and the insidious questions Tony Boswell and Brian Dawson hurled toward me before they left.

Were they all involved in the murders?

Were they trying to protect someone?

Whatever the reason might be, I was glad that I hadn't given them any information about the investigation and our thoughts as to what the killer's pattern might be.

I took in a deep breath as I closed my notepad, and put it back in my desk drawer. Then I got up and walked out of my office to go to the police station to devise a plan to catch the killer.

Chapter 46

The police station was relatively empty when I walked through the front door. A man was standing at the counter arguing about a ticket he had received earlier in the day, and a woman was sitting at one of the desks talking to an officer. Other than that the place was empty except for police officers.

As I entered, I took one step inside and stopped. I looked around the room to see if I could see Mark. He wasn't anywhere in sight, so I moved a few feet down from the man arguing and stood at the counter.

Within seconds, one of the police officers grudgingly got up from his desk and slowly walked to the counter.

"What can I help you with?" he asked in a gruff voice.

"I need to speak to Mark Stone," I said.

"What's it about?" he demanded.

"That's between me and him," I said defensively.

"Well, he's busy, and if you're not going to tell me what it's about, then I'm not going to be able to help you," he said with a smirk on his face.

I looked him in the eyes for several seconds while I tried

to decide whether I should tell him about the murders in the hospital or just keep that information to myself.

His smirk widened to a small smile as he looked back at me.

I glanced at one of the officers that sat at his desk watching our interaction with anticipation.

Then I looked back at the man and said, "It's about a case he's working on."

"Oh. Well, if you want to, I can take your statement."

"That's not what I need to talk to him about," I said exasperated. "Just tell him that Ted Maxwell is here to see him."

He stared at me for several seconds without any expression on his face. Then he leaned close to me and mumbled, "I don't take orders from civilians."

"I'm not trying to tell you what to do," I responded in a calm voice. "I just need to discuss a case he's been helping me with."

"Oh, so you're a police officer," he sarcastically said, as he looked at my hospital name tag.

"Butch, stop giving him a hard time," Mark said, as he walked into the room.

"Hey, Mark, do you know this guy?" he responded and laughed.

"Yes, I do, and I need to see him in my office," Mark said, as he stood at his door to wait for me.

"Thanks for your help," I said sarcastically to the man that Mark had called Butch. Then I walked around the counter without giving him a chance to respond.

The other officers in the squad room glanced at Mark but didn't say anything.

When I reached his office door, Mark stepped to the side

to allow me to walk in, and then he walked inside and closed the door.

"Sorry about Butch giving you trouble," Mark apologized.

"He seemed to have an attitude," I said, as I looked him in the eyes and asked, "What's his name?"

"Butch Carr," he said then continued, "He's just a little high- strung."

"Whatever he is I didn't appreciate it."

"I'll talk to him about his people skills."

"Thanks."

"What's this about?" he asked, as he walked to his desk and sat down. "Couldn't you wait until our meeting at three?"

There was a chair against the wall, so I pulled it in front of his desk and sat down.

After I got settled I announced, "I want to set a trap tonight to catch the killer."

"Wasn't that what we tried to do a few nights ago?"

"Yes, but things have changed a little bit," I said, "I've come to the conclusion that someone in management is behind the murders."

"What?" Mark exclaimed.

"I looked over each victim's chart and meticulously studied every detail in an attempt to discover a connection between the patients," I said, as I took my notepad out of my shirt pocket and continued, "After several hours, I've concluded the hospital is behind the murders solely to save money."

"That's a major accusation," Mark warned. "You'd better be ready to back up something like that with evidence."

"That's why we need to catch the killer," I said.

"I'm not saying that we don't need to catch the killer," Mark said. "But we need to have a good plan in place to catch him before we go to the hospital and scare him away."

"I have a plan," I said enthusiastically.

"But, is it a good plan?" he asked with a raised eyebrow.

"That's why I came here," I said and then explained, "I want to discuss it with you to see what you think."

"Alright, what's your plan?" he asked, as he moved up in his chair and propped his elbows on top of his desk.

I looked around his office, leaned in and quietly explained the plan I had to catch the killer.

Chapter 47

The Executioner stood hidden by the darkness in the janitor's closet to wait for the opportune time to approach his target. As he waited, he gripped the glass vial, which contained the drug he chose to use, in his right hand. He carefully turned it upside down and looked at the label.

The drug name listed on the vial was Pancuroium bromide, which is a muscle relaxant that causes complete, fast, and sustained paralysis. He took one of two syringes out of his back pocket, put it in his left hand, and withdrew 200 milligrams to be used on his target.

After recapping the needle, he put the syringe in the right inside pocket of his black jacket and threw the vial inside a large trash can that was attached to the cleaning cart. Then he repositioned the syringe to make sure he didn't stab himself before moving to the next drug.

After the Executioner was satisfied with the position of the syringe, he pulled another vial out of his pocket and turned it upside down. He looked at the label as he inserted the needle from the other syringe into the rubber stopper and began aspirating potassium chloride into the syringe.

Even though he knew 100meq of potassium chloride was sufficient to depolarize the muscle cells of the heart, which inhibits its ability to fire and eventually would stop the target's heart, he withdrew 200meq. He didn't want to take any chances, and the more he inserted the faster the target would die.

After making sure he had enough potassium chloride to do the job, he carefully recapped the syringe, making sure not to stick himself. He put it in the left inside pocket of his jacket. Then he discarded the vial in the same trash can that he used earlier and settled in the corner to wait for his chance to complete the task at hand.

Chapter 48

After discussing my plan with Mark, he suggested some revisions, which I agreed to without hesitation, such as the need for me to stay in my office throughout the process. Mark thought there was a potential that someone was watching me.

Later that night as I sat at my desk, I imagined everyone getting in place and wished I could be involved, but I knew that was unrealistic. After all, I was a civilian and the police officers were trained to handle this type of situation.

Watching the seconds tick, every minute felt like an eternity.

Feeling edgy, I got up and opened my door to see if anyone was visible, but the halls were clear.

There were three offices located on the same hall as mine. The first was George Bells', supervisor over janitorial services. The second was the office of Martha Vic, nurse manager of supplemental staffing, and the third belonged to Sherry Kirk, the woman in charge of hospital compliance for governmental affairs.

As I looked at each office door, I concentrated at the

bottom to see if any light might escape from underneath and flow out into the hallway.

The hallway was free from light, except from my office. The occupants were long gone for the night and most everyone would be home asleep.

The entire floor that my office was located on was quiet. It seemed as deserted as the ghost towns of years past. The only thing missing was the wind and the tumbleweed rolling down the hall.

After several minutes of staring down the hall for anything suspicious, I went back in my office and closed my door. Then I sat down at my desk for the excruciating wait.

Chapter 49

The Executioner inched the door open and glanced down the hall.

Nurses were scrambling with meds in their hands as they gave their scheduled medicines as well as the PRN's, meds the patients had to ask for, that were necessary to help the patients sleep.

He watched as a pharmacy tech came down the hall pushing a loaded cart. The tech headed to the med room to restock the floor's med cart with medications that would be needed for the night.

A young nurse with long blond hair opened the door to the med room and closed it without going inside. She stormed over to one of the other nurses and complained, "They always fill the med cart when we are trying to give our meds."

"I know," the other nurse said, "That's why I get my meds out at the beginning of the shift."

"What about your PRN meds?" the blond asked.

"I know I'm going to give them something to help them sleep, so I got that out, too," she said smugly. Then she sobered up and added, "But if I need anything else like pain meds, then I have to wait for the pharmacy tech to leave."

"They should come after our scheduled med times," the blond insisted.

"I know, but they're not worried about us or that we need to give our patients their meds," she said and walked away with a cup full of meds in her right hand.

The Executioner eased the door closed and leaned against the wall to wait for the nurses to finish giving the patients their medicines.

He pushed the button on the side of his watch to illuminate the screen.

It was now eleven o'clock.

His plan was to take the target out by eleven thirty and be out of the hospital before midnight, but with the nurses' delay in giving medications he would be an hour behind schedule. He placed his right hand on one of the syringes and thought with frustration, I should take them out in the process.

He closed his eyes and thought back to the time when he killed Susan Brunner. As he ran the scene through his mind, he marveled over the excitement he felt as he saw her life slowly leaving her body.

And he realized the excitement that he once felt when he took out his targets had slowly diminished. Since he was being told which person to kill, the motivation was somewhat lessened. He now looked at it as a job. It was just another way to earn a dollar. Yes, he was helping the hospital, but his desire was slowly fading.

Chapter 50

Officer Mary Ward, wearing pale gray scrubs and a white lab coat that she had borrowed from one of the night shift nurses, stood at the nurses' desk. She vigilantly watched for the killer as she waited for everyone to give their medicines. Before the shift began, she had instructed everyone to act as they always do and give the same nursing care to the patients that they do every day.

However, there was a small glitch when the pharmacy tech came early to deliver meds, which delayed the nurse's ability to follow the plan.

Mary tried not to look perturbed, but her tension was rising and her patience was wearing thin as she looked at her watch then glanced at the clock to compare times.

She thought, the tech must leave, and she slowly started walking toward the med room.

The door opened when she reached for the doorknob, and the pharmacy tech walked out with her cell phone still attached to her ear. She didn't notice Mary because she was too engrossed in her conversation to realize anyone else was around.

Mary watched as she rolled her cart down the hall and disappeared around the corner. She then turned to the two nurses still waiting to give meds and whispered, "Quickly give your meds because we are behind schedule."

They looked at the clock in unison then one of the nurses said, "Alright we'll be as quick as we can," and they both went into the med room together.

All the meds were passed out by midnight and the lights were dimmed in the hall to promote a more relaxed atmosphere.

After everything was done, the last two nurses paused at the front of the desk for a few seconds before moving around to the back and sitting down at the computers.

Mary quickly glanced down the hall then said in a loud voice, "After we're finished charting we'll order supper," and she walked to the back of the nurses' desk where the other nurses were sitting.

When she got to the back, she leaned against the wall with her eyes focused on the front of the nurses' desk and her right hand resting lightly on her Glock 9mm that was inside her lab coat pocket.

She glanced periodically at the nurses as they nervously charted on their patients. Occasionally someone would tell a joke as they tried to maintain the same relaxed attitude that they displayed every night.

As they continued charting, one of the nurses asked, "What do y'all want to eat?"

"I don't know," someone said then asked, "What's open at this time of night?"

"We'll check on that after we get through charting," the first nurse said.

Everyone was quiet for a few minutes, but then they began

discussing their patients and what was wrong with them.

As they talked, Mary refocused her attention on the dimly lit hall and the killer that might approach at any time.

Chapter 51

The Executioner pressed the illuminating button on his watch to check the time. It was now twelve thirty in the morning, and if everything was normal the nurses would be charting in the back of the nurses' station.

After his watch light went off, he inched the door open and stood looking toward the nurses' desk for several minutes. When no one appeared, he stepped out into the hall and pressed himself against the wall, listening for footsteps.

He could hear the nurses talking in the distance. They were nowhere near him, but he could hear them clearly. According to their conversation, they weren't concerned about him at all. They were gossiping and talking about where they were going to eat.

Staying close to the wall the Executioner slowly and quietly moved toward the nurses' desk. He paused as he reached the counter and peeped around toward the back where the nurses were sitting.

They were in deep conversation and not aware of anyone else.

He took a deep breath, bent down, and quickly darted past

the nurse's desk. As he got past, he stood up and ran toward the back hall, stopping a few feet before turning the corner.

He took his handkerchief out of his pocket, poured a generous amount of chloroform in the center and rushed around the corner ready to cuff it over the nurse's nose and mouth if one was stationed in the back.

He stopped in his tracks when he saw that the computer desk was empty and plastered his body against the wall as he rubbed the sweat off his forehead with his shirt sleeve.

Warning signals when off in his head. No one was stationed in the back. He rationalized the situation by thinking they were afraid to leave a nurse alone on the back hall, and he decided to continue with the plan.

His heart was pounding.

The excitement was mounting. The adrenaline was flowing.

Reaching inside the left side of his jacket, he wrapped his hand around the syringe filled with potassium. Then he felt for the right side to make sure he still had the syringe of Pancuroium bromide and smiled as they both were still just as he had left them.

The Executioner thought back to earlier in the day when he had walked by his target's room and saw two IV's with fluids infusing in each arm. He remembered the excitement he felt because he wanted to execute someone in the manner that death row inmates were put to death. He knew potassium chloride and Pancuroium bromide couldn't be mixed. During his research, he discovered that mixing the two would precipitate and clog the needle, so two IV's were imperative.

As he walked toward his target's room, he looked around to make sure no one was watching. He stopped outside the door for a few seconds before stepping inside.

The room was dark with only a glimmer of light spilling over the curtain.

The Executioner stepped to the foot of the bed and stood looking at his next victim. IV fluid was still infusing in each arm with the help of two IV pumps. One pump was set at 75cc an hour and the other was set at 10cc an hour.

He reached inside his jacket and pulled out the syringe filled with the muscle relaxant. Then he slowly stepped to the left side with the syringe in his hand.

"Who are you?" asked the victim in a sleepy voice.

"I'm Doctor Lang," the Executioner said, "I have some medicine to give you."

"Where's my nurse?" he asked. "Doctors never give medicine."

"Your nurse was busy, so I told her I would give it," the Executioner said, as he moved close to the victim's IV line and attached the syringe.

The target didn't say anything else; he just watched as the killer began pushing the contents of the syringe into the line.

As the muscle relaxant began to enter the target's blood stream, he closed his eyes.

The Executioner finished emptying the syringe. Then he went to the right side and turned the pump off. He took the syringe filled with potassium chloride out of his jacket and pushed it into the IV as fast as he could. Then he turned the pump back on and increased the volume to 75cc an hour to get the potassium into his heart to stop it from beating.

He watched the target for several minutes, and then he turned to walk out the door.

Chapter 52

The suspect stopped in midstride when the lights came on and a deep voice from behind him demanded, "Don't take another step."

He slowly put his foot down and hesitantly turned around to find his victim, which he had given enough potassium and muscle relaxant to kill an elephant, sitting up in the bed with a gun pointing directly at him.

A cold sweat enveloped his body as he looked in the bed where two artificial arms were lying with IV tubing inserted into each one and realized he had stepped into a trap.

Mark Stone emerged from the shadows with his gun extended and announced, "You're under arrest. Put your hands behind your back."

The man smiled and turned toward the door and took a step.

"You don't want to do that," Butch Carr threatened, as he stepped inside the room and raised his Glock 9mm.

As he looked down the barrel of the massive gun that Butch was holding, the man stopped and quickly took a step back inside the room.

"I was just checking on the patient," the suspect said defensively.

"You didn't just check on the patient," Mark said, "You pushed drugs through the IV."

"I was checking his IV line," he responded. "I didn't push any drugs."

"I saw you," Mark said with irritation in his voice.

"It was dark. How could you see anything?" he rebuked.

"I saw enough to place you under arrest," Mark said, as he grabbed the suspect's right arm and put a cuff across his wrist.

"You can't do that," the suspect yelled.

"He can do whatever he pleases," Butch said, as he put his hand on the suspect's chest and pushed him back a step. "Now, put your left arm behind your back," he added matter-of-factly.

He stared at Butch for a few seconds, but then he slowly moved his left arm behind his back without saying another word.

Mark grabbed the suspect's arm and connected the other handcuff to it.

"What's your name?" Mark asked.

"I want a lawyer," he responded.

"You can call your lawyer when you get to the police station."

"Fine, then I'll talk when I get to the police station," he said defiantly.

Mark shook his head as he looked at the suspect and said under his breath, "Have it your way."

"You're not helping yourself by not speaking," Butch said scornfully.

"Well, I'm not hurting myself either," the suspect said.

"Butch, take him out in the hall and read him his rights," Mark said as he made sure the handcuffs were tight.

"I didn't do anything wrong," the man protested and tried to pull his hands apart.

"If you pull against those cuffs, you're going to hurt your wrist," Butch said, as he took the suspect by the right arm and added, "Come with me peacefully, and we'll have no problems."

The man stared at Butch for several seconds. Then he turned his head with a defiant look and slowly started walking toward the door.

As they walked, Butch began to quote the Miranda rights to his prisoner.

"Don't move out of the bed until the CSI crew can gather evidence," Mark instructed, as he looked at the man that pretended to be the patient. Then he took his cell phone out of his pocket and continued, "I need to call Ted and let him know that we've caught the killer."

Mark moved to the edge of the room as Justin Wells stepped inside and sat his evidence case against the wall.

He punched in some numbers and turned to the wall as he waited for his call to be answered.

Chapter 53

I glanced at the clock as I paced around my office. Then I sighed as I realized it had only been five minutes since the last time I had looked and over an hour past the time I thought the killer would be caught.

As time slowly ticked away, my anxiety level intensified and doubts began to run through my mind. Did the killer know about the plan? Is more than one person involved in the murders? How far up the chain of command do the murders go?

I was about to start answering my questions or at least debating with myself when my phone started ringing.

After the second ring, I picked it up and blurted out, "Ted speaking."

"We have the killer," Mark declared.

"Great!" I said with excitement then asked, "Who was he?"

"He wouldn't give me his name, but he was in the ICU when we came to investigate the last murder."

"Really."

"Yes, I don't remember which one he was, but he was on

the floor."

"Is he still up there?"

"Yes, Butch has him in the hall reading him his rights."

"Keep him there, and I'll see you in a minute," I said, as I put the phone down on the receiver and ran out the door.

I bypassed the elevator and burst through the door to the stairs. Taking two steps at a time, I ran up the stairs without stopping to catch my breath.

When I reached the floor, I rushed through the door into the hall. Slowing my pace to a brisk walk, I quickly went to the nurses' desk.

Butch Carr was standing in the hall with a man pushed against the wall.

As I looked around the floor for Mark, I saw him emerge from the room across from where Butch and the man were standing. I hurried down toward him.

When I got close, Mark pointed across the hall and asked, "Do you know him?"

I looked at the man that was standing with Butch, but he had his back to me and refused to turn around.

"Turn around so they can see your face," Butch ordered, as he grabbed his right arm and pulled him around to face us.

The man stared at me for a few seconds without saying anything. Then he looked away.

"Are you sure he's the killer?" I asked in amazement as I looked at Mark.

"I saw him inject the IV with two things. Justin should be able to tell us what he was using shortly."

"Why?" I asked, as I turned to the man.

"Why?" he repeated. "Why not?" he said and smiled.

"We're supposed to save lives."

"Some lives aren't worth saving," he said, as he turned to

Butch and added, "If you're taking me to jail, then let's go."

"Take him away," Mark said to Butch. "I'll book him when I get there."

"Let's go," Butch instructed as he led him down the hall.

A lady dressed in gray scrubs met them at the nurses' desk and walked with them off the floor.

After they disappeared, Mark and I went to the door and watched as Justin gathered evidence.

He had two glass containers filled with a liquid material, one clear and one white in color, which he had taken from the artificial arms. He placed both containers in his evidence box to be transported to the lab. A sharps container had been taken off the wall and was standing beside his evidence gathering kit.

Roger Farris was dusting the infusion pumps for fingerprints and collecting the tubing to take back to the lab.

"Did you know the killer?" Mark asked.

"Yes, his name is Brian Dawson," I answered. "He's the director over the Department of Surgery."

"So, he's one of the directors in the hospital."

"Yes, he is."

"How did you know he would target a victim on rehab 5?" Mark asked, as we watched Justin searching for more evidence.

"I was looking at his pattern," I said then explained, "He had killed two patients on 3N, two patients in the ICU, and only one on rehab 5. Plus, three of the patients in rehab didn't have insurance and had been in the hospital for several weeks."

"That's the three rooms you wanted us to be in," Mark said, as he slowly shook his head, understanding the reasoning behind my plan.

"It is," I confirmed. "I wasn't sure which room he would pick, but I was almost certain that one of the three patients would be his target."

"Do you think he did it on his own?"

"No, I think someone else was involved."

"When I get back to the police station, I'll interrogate him and see if I can get any information."

"Do you think he'll talk?"

"We have ways to persuade people to say more than they want to," Mark said, as he moved back to allow enough room for Justin and Roger to step out into the hall.

"We'll run some tests on the evidence we've collected when we get back to the lab," Justin said.

"Did you find much?" I asked with anticipation.

"We have the substance that he injected into the IV lines and that should be enough to charge him with attempted murder."

"What about the sharps container?" I asked, as I looked at Roger who was holding it in his right hand.

"We'll carefully go through it and see if we can find the syringes," Justin said, "They should have a trace of the substance he used and his fingerprints on them."

I turned to the room when a man dressed in a hospital gown stepped out into the hall and asked, "Can I get dressed now?"

"Oh, I'm sorry Robert," Mark said, "Yes, you need to get dressed so we can go to the police station."

"Thanks," he said and went back into the room.

"Who was that?" I asked.

Mark smiled then said, "That was Robert Cook. He played the part of the patient."

"Why was he still dressed in a gown?"

"I told him not to move until they finished gathering evidence."

"Oh."

"He's a good cop and follows orders."

"Listen guys, we got to get back to the CSI lab to start working on this evidence," Justin said.

"Thanks for helping," I said.

"We're happy to do it," Justin said over his shoulder as he was walking away.

"Mark, we'll call you as soon as we have the results," Roger said then he followed Justin off the floor.

Robert emerged from the room fully dressed and stood beside Mark.

"Robert, now that you're ready we need to go," Mark said with a smirk.

"You told me not to move," Robert said defensively.

"I know," he said, "I was just kidding."

"Mark, I really appreciate you getting all the police involved so we could catch this killer," I said.

"That's what we do," Mark said, as he shook my hand and added, "I'll call you this afternoon," and he walked off the floor.

I watched them as they disappeared into the elevator then I walked inside the room where the killer was caught. The room was a mess from the CSI crew gathering evidence, but by early morning it would be clean and ready for another patient. With no one knowing what had occurred during the night.

After taking a deep breath, I walked out of the room and went home.

Chapter 54

Mark Stone walked into the police station with determination in his stride. He glanced at Butch who was standing at the counter and said, "Bring the prisoner into the conference room."

"Are you not going to book him first?" Butch asked.

"I can fill out the paperwork after we talk to him."

"Alright, I'll get him," he said, as he walked out of the squad room.

Mark stopped at the desk where Robert Cook was sitting and said, "I want you to help with the interrogation."

"Are we going to be rough on him?" Robert asked.

"If we have to in order to get the information we need," Mark said solemnly. "I think someone else was helping him, and I want to know who it was."

"Do you think he'll talk," he asked, as he got up and walked around his desk.

"We'll soon find out," Mark answered, and they walked to the conference room.

Robert turned the lights on, and we stepped inside the conference room. A twenty feet oblong solid oak table sat in the middle of the room surrounded by several leather office chairs.

"Let's get the room ready for the prisoner," Mark said as he walked to the closet.

Robert began pushing everything against the wall. He left two high back executive chairs facing the door for us to sit in.

Mark took a folding metal chair out of the closet and placed it at the table for the suspect to sit in and said, "One of the key rules to interrogating a prisoner is to make them as uncomfortable as possible."

"And for us to look comfortable," Robert added and laughed.

"The less stressed we look the more stressed he'll be."

"Do you want me to get him a bottle of water?" Robert asked as he took a step toward the refrigerator.

"No, that's something we'll offer him during the questioning to possibly make him more cooperative," Mark said as he sat down at the table.

Robert sat down beside him to wait for Butch to bring the prisoner.

Chapter 55

We had just gotten everything ready and sat down when Butch opened the door. He had a firm grip on the prisoner's right arm and was partly dragging him as they walked into the room.

"I can walk! You don't have to drag me!" the prisoner yelled.

"Then move a little faster," Butch barked, as he led him to the metal chair and ordered, "Sit down."

He hesitated for a few seconds as he looked at the metal chair, and then he sat down without saying anything.

Mark sat up straight, leaned his elbows on the table to get as close to the prisoner as possible and asked, "What's your name?"

"Where's my lawyer?" he responded.

"Look, I know your name is Brian Dawson."

"Then, why did you ask if you already knew my name?"

"It's a way to start the questioning, but if you're not willing to cooperate, I'm not going to be able to help you."

"Help me," he said, as he looked scornfully across the table. "How could you possibly help me?" he asked sarcastically.

Mark leaned in and said, "I might be able to keep you off death row."

"As I said earlier, I've done nothing wrong."

"I witnessed you trying to kill a patient."

"I didn't try to kill anybody," he said, "I was checking on the patient."

"When does a master's degree in business administration qualify you to take care of a patient in the hospital?"

"I didn't do anything wrong."

"Look, Brian," Mark said, as he moved a little closer. "We were able to remove the drugs from the artificial arms and, as we speak, are having them analyzed at the CSI lab. Robert and I both saw you inject the drugs into the IV tubing. You may not believe it, but the courts will believe two cops over a hospital director, and you will go to jail. You don't have to go down alone. If you cooperate I can help you."

Brian Dawson dropped his head and remained quiet for several minutes as he suddenly realized they had enough evidence to put him away for several years if not put him on death row. Then he looked up and asked, "What do you want from me?"

"Who was behind the murders?"

"I need confirmation that the DA will take the death penalty away."

"I called the DA on the way to the police station and she assured me that she wouldn't seek the death penalty if you cooperated."

"I want it in writing."

"I thought you would say that so I asked her to fax a statement over to that affect," Mark said as he turned to Butch and said, "Go check the fax machine and see if it's gotten here yet."

"Sure," Butch said and he walked out the door.

"Do you want a bottle of water," Mark asked, as he got up and went to the refrigerator.

"I guess," Brian said hesitantly.

Everyone turned to the door as it opened, and Butch stepped inside with a single sheet of paper in his hand.

He held it up and announced, "I have it."

"Let me see it," Brian said, as he held his hand out.

Butch looked at Mark who was standing with the refrigerator door open.

"Did you make a copy of it?" Mark asked.

"Yes, and I left it on your desk," he answered.

"Alright, hand him the paper and let him read it."

Butch gave Brian the paper, and then he backed away and stood against the wall.

After looking over the paper, Brian laid it on top of the table and conceded, "I'll tell you everything I know."

Mark placed the water in front of Brian, and then he walked around the table and sat down to begin the questioning.

Brian eagerly discussed each victim and gave a complete detail of the murders. He seemed to relish the attention as he controlled the situation and talked almost nonstop for over an hour.

When he got to the night he was caught he sat back, held his hands out in a questioning manner, and said, "You know about last night."

"Who helped you pick the victims?" Mark asked.

He moved close to the table and whispered, "I got my instructions from Kelly Adams, Larry Adcock's assistant, but I assume they came from Larry."

"Did you ever get any instructions directly from him?"

"No," he said and he lowered his head.

"Why did you kill Leo Brown and Susan Brunner?"

"Susan Brunner was just in the wrong place at the wrong time," he said, as he thought back. "She stayed on the back hall by the stairwell and blocked the way I entered the floor. And Leo Brown got in my way as I was gathering material to use on the targets. I think he saw me get a box of syringes off the cart, and he possibly saw me when I put the box of normal saline with heparin on his cart. He was just becoming too familiar with me, and I was afraid he would put two and two together and tell anyone that might listen."

"So, Kelly Adams didn't tell you to kill them?"

"No, they were just casualties of the mission."

"Butch, take him back to his cell," Mark said as he stood up. "I need to go talk to Kelly Adams," and he walked to his office to call the DA.

After getting an arrest warrant for Kelly Adams, he went into the squad room and said, "Robert, I need you and Bill to follow me to the hospital," then he walked out the door.

Chapter 56

Mark walked into my office followed by two of his officers and announced, "Dawson confessed to the murders."

"Really," I said with surprise, as I looked up from the computer.

"Yeah, he seemed to enjoy giving an extensive description of how he killed each victim."

"Did he sign his confession?"

"No, but I recorded it," Mark said. "I'll type it up when I get back to the station and have him sign it."

"What if he refuses?" I asked.

"Justin called me as I drove over here and gave me a report on the evidence they gathered at the crime scene," he said, as he sat down in front of my desk. "One of the chemicals Dawson injected into the IV was potassium chloride, and the other was a muscle relaxant called Pancuroium bromide. He also found the syringes Dawson used, and they had his fingerprints all over them."

"How did they know which syringes he used?"

"They were the only 30cc syringes in the sharps container and with the medication he had been giving the victims,

Justin determined that a bigger syringe had to have been used."

"That's enough evidence to convict him of attempted murder, but what if he doesn't sign his confession."

"Justin and Roger are comparing the evidence gathered last night with what was gathered from the other victims to see if anything matches," Mark said, "I can still use the recording if I need to."

"Did he explain why he was killing people?"

"He said it started out as a game. A way to get his adrenaline flowing. He enjoyed the excitement of locating his victims in the hospital and planning different ways to kill them that resembled natural causes. Then one day when he was in the pharmacy stealing medications to use, Kelly Adams walked in and confronted him. She threatened to call the police if he didn't start targeting the people she instructed him to target."

"Which were patients without insurance," I said.

"Yes," Mark said, "She gave him the name of the patient she wanted him to kill and a deadline in which to accomplish the murder."

"So, she basically ran the show."

"Dawson seemed to think that Larry Adcock was behind the names she gave him. He had made a speech in one of their meetings about the drain the uninsured were on the hospital. He had challenged everyone to come up with a plan to get them out of the hospital as fast as they could."

"I don't believe that," I said flatly, "He was adamant that we catch the killer because it was making the hospital look bad."

"I'm not accusing him," Mark said, "I'm just repeating what Dawson said."

"So, Kelly Adams was the reason Dawson targeted the uninsured," I said.

"That's what he said."

"Are you going to arrest her?"

"That's why we stopped by here," Mark said, "I want you to go with us to arrest her."

"Why?"

"Because you know the hospital better than I do," Mark said. "I want to go straight to her office and arrest her without making a scene."

"The hospital is already in an uproar because Brian Dawson was arrested last night," I said, "And this could infuriate the hospital management."

"Well, I don't want to make it any worse," Mark said, "But we've got to arrest her."

"I know."

"I need you to go with us so we can keep it quiet."

"Sure, I'll go," I said as I stood up.

"You do know what she looks like don't you."

"I'd recognize her if I saw her."

"Good. Let's go," Mark said as he got up and opened the door.

We walked out into the hall on our way to the administration offices.

Chapter 57

The administration offices were relatively empty. All the lights in the hall were dim, and several rooms were completely dark.

Kelly Adams' office was located beside Larry Adcock's which was at the end of the hall beside the stairwell.

As we rounded the corner, we walked as quietly as we could trying not to draw any attention to our presence.

I pointed at a tiny strip of light that emerged from under the door at the end of the hall and whispered, "That's Larry Adcock's office."

"He looks like the only one here," Mark whispered.

"I know," I said in a low voice. "I guess they got spooked after Dawson was arrested."

"They have no reason to be spooked unless they are involved."

When we got to Kelly Adams' office, I walked inside and turned the lights on. I touched the computer, which was still cold. Then I went to the copy machine, and it was cold. Her answering machine had a red light flashing an indicator that she had a message, so I hit the play button.

A male voice wanted to clarify what time he was to meet with Larry Adcock next week. Mark looked at me when the answering machine announced that the call had been received at eight o'clock this morning, which indicated that Kelly Adams hadn't been at work today.

"Do you know where she lives?" Mark asked in a low voice.

"No," I said, "We'll have to ask Mr. Adcock to give us her address."

"Do you think he will?"

"You may have to get a search warrant."

"I will if I have to."

"Let's go talk to him and see what he says," I said as I went into the hall and knocked on his door.

Within a minute, Larry Adcock opened the door and looked at us questioningly. Then he looked me in the eyes and asked, "Ted, what's going on here?"

"As you've heard Brian Dawson was arrested this morning," I responded.

"Yes, what's that got to do with me?"

I looked at Mark without answering.

"Tell him what we need," Mark said.

"Dawson indicated that Kelly Adams was behind some of the murders. Since she's not here, we need her home address."

Mr. Adcock looked at the two officers behind us, and then he looked at Mark and asked, "Do you have a warrant for her arrest?"

"Yes I do," Mark said as he took it out of his pocket.

"Well, she didn't show up for work today, and I haven't heard anything from her," he said as he thought for a second. Then he added, "She normally calls me when she can't come to work."

"Did you not get worried?" I asked.

"To tell you the truth, I've had my mind on other things this morning."

"Such as the murders in the hospital," I said.

"Yes, they've occupied my mind today."

"Do you have her address?" Mark asked.

"Oh, yes. She lives in the Oakridge Apartments on Valley Road," he said as he walked to his desk and looked at his rolodex. "Apartment number 416."

"Thank you," I said.

"I just hope she's okay," he said.

"I do too."

He looked uncomfortable as he looked at us, and then he asked, "Is there anything else?"

"Yes, I'd like to ask a few questions about Mrs. Adams if you don't mind," Mark said as he took a step closer.

"What kind of questions?" Larry Adcock asked suspiciously.

"How long has she worked for the hospital?"

"Let's see, she has been my assistant for about ten years and before that she worked on 3N as a secretary for about five years, so I guess she's worked for the hospital for about fifteen years total."

"Why did she leave 3N?"

"Her and the nurse manager had a difference in opinion and she was about to quit when I asked her to come work for me."

"You gave her a promotion to keep her from quitting?" I asked in disbelief.

"Her grandparents donated a lot of money to the hospital, and I did it as a favor to them," he said, "In fact, the Neal and Fanny Adams sports facility located beside the rehab gym was almost completely paid for by her grandparents."

"Was she a good worker?"

"Yes, she scheduled my meetings by location so I could make them in a timely manner. She filtered my calls and directed them to the person that it should go too which eliminated a lot on unnecessary calls from vendors giving me a lot more time to do my job. And she almost never missed a day of work. In fact, I think she might be more devoted to the hospital than my directors are."

"Is she married?"

"No, I don't think she's ever dated anybody," he answered. "When she's not at work she's at her grandmother's helping take care of her."

"Did the directors know that she was your assistant because of her grandparents and their money?" I asked.

"No, that was between me and her."

"How did she get along with the directors?"

"Good, I think," he said hesitantly. "She treated them professionally, but she worked for me and she made that known to them. If they asked her to do something for them she always told them to get my permission first."

"Has she been acting strange lately?" Mark asked.

He took a deep breath, let it out slowly then said, "I don't know if you'd call it strange, but recently she's really been getting angry when we go over the hospital's budget. Especially when I discussed my concerns about the new healthcare plan and the hospital's increased number of patients that are unable to pay their bills."

"What did she say?" I asked.

"She said the deadbeat patients were going to bankrupt the hospital her grandparents loved and she was going to do whatever it took to make sure that didn't happen."

"Did she tell you how she planned on doing that?"

"No, she didn't tell me how she was going to save the hospital," he said. "I thought she was just letting out some steam."

"Well, apparently she wasn't," Mark interjected.

"I've told you everything I know," Larry Adcock said as he sat back in his chair and asked, "Is there anything else?"

"No, that's it," I said.

"Good, because I need to get back to work."

"Thanks for the information," Mark said, as we turned and walked away.

I heard the door close before we got halfway down the hall.

"He didn't seem to be too upset," Mark said, as he glanced over his shoulder.

"No, he seemed preoccupied," I said.

"That might have been it," Mark said, as we got on the elevator.

"I hope this is the end of the murders," I said as I stepped off the elevator to go to my office.

"I'll call you when I get back to the police station," Mark yelled, as the door closed.

I stood there for a few seconds before I turned and went to my office to document the information that Mark had given me.

Chapter 58

I jumped as someone knocked on my door. Then I got up and cautiously opened it.

As the door opened, I saw Mark Stone leaning against the door frame with a frown on his face.

"I thought you were going to call me from the police station," I said as I moved to the side to allow him to walk inside my office.

"I was, but it took so long at Kelly Adams' home that I thought I would come by and fill you in on what's been happening," Mark said, and he sat down in the first chair he came to.

"What happened?"

"After knocking several times on her door and not getting an answer, I got the superintendent to open it."

"Did he give you a hard time?"

"Not after I showed him the search warrant."

"Was she home?"

"You might say that," Mark said with an odd look on his face. "She was hanging from the ceiling."

"She hung herself?"

"Yes, she wrapped a sheet around one of the rafters in her kitchen and jumped off the table."

"Did she leave a note?"

Mark said, "Yes, she left it on the kitchen counter," as he took a sheet of paper, that had been placed in a plastic bag, out of his shirt pocket and laid it on top of my desk.

I picked up the plastic covered paper and began reading,

BY NOW, YOU KNOW ABOUT THE ARRANGEMENT I HAD WITH BRIAN DAWSON. I TAKE FULL CREDIT FOR MY ACTIONS. I BELIEVE IT'S BEST FOR ME TO END MY LIFE RATHER THAN SUBJECT MYSELF AND MY FAMILY TO THE HUMILIATION OF GOING TO TRIAL. EVERYTHING I DID WAS IN THE BEST INTEREST OF THE HOSPITAL. WITH ALL THE MONEY MY GRANDPARENTS DONATED TO THE HOSPITAL, I COULDN'T SIT BACK AND ALLOW IT TO FALL INTO BANKRUPTCY I WANT TO EMPHASIZE THAT LARRY ADCOCK, WHO I THOUGHT OF AS A FATHER BECAUSE HE ALWAYS LOOKED OUT FOR MY WELL-BEING AND THE REST OF THE HOSPITAL STAFF AND WHO ALWAYS TREATED ME WITH KINDNESS AND RESPECT, HAD NO KNOWLEDGE OF THE MURDERS. I LOOK BACK AND REGRET THAT PEOPLE HAD TO DIE, BUT THE LEECHES OF SOCIETY WERE SLOWLY DRAINING THE RESOURCES FROM THE HOSPITAL. I HAD TO GET THEIR ATTENTION. I APOLOGIZE TO THOSE I'VE HURT, BUT REST ASSURED THAT I'LL NEVER DO IT AGAIN.

WITH DEEP SORROW,

KELLY ADAMS

I laid the note on my desk and covered my face with my hands. After taking several deep breaths, I lowered my hands and asked, "Are you sure she wrote the note?"

"I got the CSI crew to come by to investigate, but I think she did," Mark answered as he picked the letter up and put it back in his pocket.

"Could you tell how long she had been dead?"

"Glen Watts came by to get the body," Mark said, "And he estimated that she had been dead since early this morning."

"I guess she knew that Dawson would talk."

"I guess so."

"Where does that leave you with Dawson's confession?"

"I had Butch type up the confession and have Dawson sign it when I found the body," Mark said, "I thought it was better to have that done before he found out she was dead."

"Do you think the DA's going to try to get the death penalty for Dawson?"

"No," he answered. "I made a deal with him, and he stuck to his part so I'm going to stick to mine."

"I think he should be executed," I said.

"I understand you have an opinion, but that's not your call," Mark argued.

"I know, but he killed seven innocent people and he deserves to die the same way they did."

"Ted, I don't disagree," Mark said as he stood up. "But that's for the courts to decide," and he walked out the door.

I looked at the open door for several seconds before turning my attention back to my computer. As I sat looking at the screen, I felt an overwhelming sense of relief. The killers were caught, and the murders would finally be stopped.

After several minutes of not being able to concentrate, I got up and went home with the satisfied feeling that the patients would now be safe.

About the Author

Joseph J. Landers was born in 1962 in rural Alabama. He's married and has four kids. While pursuing his nursing degree, he studied English composition and American literature. After several years of nursing, his interest in writing continued to grow and he began to focus his attention toward developing good clean novels. He has two published books, *Our Deadly Sins* and *Drug Revenge*.

FEEDBACK REQUEST

Thank you for purchasing my book. I hope you have enjoyed reading it as much as I enjoyed writing it. Please take a few minutes to leave a review for my book on Amazon.com.

Simply visit Amazon.com and insert the in the search box and my book will come right up.

Feel free to express your thoughts and feelings both positive and otherwise. I deeply appreciate your feedback. While you are there, you may notice what others thought of my book as well; perhaps your insights are shared with others.

Thank you in advance for taking the time to respond. I will check Amazon.com soon to read your response.

Made in the USA
San Bernardino, CA
16 October 2013